Praise for the author...

Namou is a patient and subtle writer who instills trust in the reader bit by bit.

—The 13th Warrior Review

Weam Namou's language is incredibly fresh and enticing. She will make quite a splash in the literary pond.

—Elizabeth Sikander, Poet

This groundbreaking author brings the old customs and ways of life to the modern world.

—Charley Gray Wolf, Ph.D.

HERMiZ
PUBLiSHING

Hermiz Publishing, Inc.

Copyright © 2006 by Weam Namou

ISBN 0-9776790-0-4 (paperback)

Library of Congress Cataloging-in-Publication Data:
2006927065

10 9 8 7 6 5 4 3 2 1

First Edition

Published in the United States of America by:
Hermiz Publishing, Inc.
P.O. Box 4672
Troy, MI 48099 USA
www.HermizPublishing.com
Email: info@HermizPublishing.com

For my loving husband,
and our lovely daughter

Weam Namou

The Mismatched Braid

A Hermiz Publishing Book

CHAPTER 1

Amel Aboona sanded the wood in anger. Yesterday, for the second time, his application for a visa for America was rejected. Now he would have to spend another winter in Athens. He didn't care how the chair he was building turned out—whether it had four or five legs, toes or a chin. Let them fire him, even ship him back to Baghdad, he thought. He would take fighting in a war any day over the tortures of living in a foreign land.

He saw his boss coming and broke into a sweat. A nail stuck out the wrong side of the board. He quickly scanned the floor for a hammer. He found it by Adel's foot, went to grab it but tripped over a half-completed bedpost. Wiping dust off his knees, he heard the name given him by his Greek associates.

"Demitri," his boss called over the loud machinery.

"*Ti?*" Amel asked.

"*Tilefono.* It's your mother."

Amel rushed to get the telephone before it disconnected. Since the Gulf War, outgoing calls from Baghdad were limited to five minutes. He barely said hello before his mother started weeping – she had heard the bad news and this was her way of consoling him. "*Youm,* you'd better tell *Babba* to talk with his brothers in America," he threatened in Chaldean, the language of Christian Iraqis who originated from Mesopotamia. "If they don't get me out of Greece soon, I'm going back to Iraq."

She wept harder.

"The first time I got rejected, my uncles promised to write me such a convincing story, I'd be granted a visa. Now I'm rejected a second time! Second rejections are final. This means I'm stuck here forever."

"What if you go to Rome? The embassy there...."

"I don't want to go to Rome!"

"Alright, don't upset yourself," she said, her tears suddenly gone. "Amel, I must tell you something before the line cuts off. My niece Dunia is flying into Athens in a couple of days. She's taking college courses there. I want you to take good care of her, like you would your own sister."

He laughed bitterly. One minute his mother tore her hair out over his despair, the next minute she clobbered him with responsibilities. He needed to get a hold of someone who understood the trouble he was in, like a psychiatrist or the President of the United States. Clinton looked like a reasonable guy.

"You must think I'm on vacation here," he said. "I work twelve, fourteen-hour shifts. I barely have time to sleep much less play host."

There was dead silence, then a dial tone. He slammed the phone down and looked around to see if his boss or coworkers noticed. He checked the phone for damage. The phone okay, he punched the wall. He studied his knuckles for scratches or bruises.

Since childhood, he had understood America was his future, his escape from war. His family's plan was to get him out of Baghdad before he finished twelfth grade. The Gulf War changed that. Travel was closed so tightly that even birds couldn't cross the border.

The safest route to smuggle him out was through Turkey to Greece, where, it was said, the American embassy granted refugees visas. In this way, he separated from his family for the first time. A Czechoslovakian smuggler led him and a group of thirteen others in the dark across forests and borders. The others—with children in their arms and signs of age—made him count his blessings despite the dangers and hardships they endured.

Amel had left the last vestige of his boyhood behind him halfway through those foreign lands. The person he was now existed only in his parents' hearts.

His cousin Sabah approached him. At twenty-two, he was only a few years older than Amel, but already balding. Amel had thick hair, and although he was only twenty, quite a few gray hairs were mixed in with the black—half of them inherited from his father, the other half from his anxieties. Both men were 5' 7" and slender. Sabah had kept his moustache, but Amel had shaved his off right after arriving in Greece. He wanted to blend in with the Europeans. Yet his thick brows, dark skin, hairy arms and mangling of Greek words revealed his Middle Eastern heritage.

"All is well with your family?" Sabah asked in Arabic. Both born and raised in Baghdad, they were more at ease speaking Arabic than Chaldean. Their parents, having come from the Chaldean village of Telkaif in Northern Iraq, were the opposite.

Amel snarled. He wanted to grab Sabah's neck like a tube of toothpaste and squeeze out the grin on his face. Being denied a visa was not funny. He should either be given special treatment or shot. Other options were out of the question. He didn't want to sneak into another country again and endure climbing high mountains and rough terrain, braving dogs, armed soldiers and government officials. The end of it was his favorite part: in the middle of the night, in clothes filthier than month-old bed pans, being dropped off at a stranger's house, a so and so's friend of a so and so's husband.

He tried to eat lunch alone, but Sabah wouldn't hear of it. He sat close beside him and asked if he had heard the joke about the priest and police officer. Amel didn't reply.

"There was a police officer who absolutely loved giving people tickets," Sabah said, biting into his green apple. "He used to give seventy to a hundred tickets a day. So people filed complaints against him until the chief officer took him out of that district. He placed him in the desert, where he couldn't bother anyone. The police officer couldn't find a single person to ticket, so he was itching for action. One day at midnight, he sees a priest driving a bicycle. He stops him and asks why he's out so late. The priest says he'd just finished mass and was on his way home.

"'Aren't you afraid of driving this late at night?' the policeman asked.

"'Why should I be afraid, my son? I have the Virgin Mary behind me and Jesus Christ in front of me.'

"'What!?' said the policeman. 'You're driving three people on one bicycle!' And gave him a ticket."

Amel didn't smile. Sabah gobbled the apple's core, then picked his teeth with its stem.

"Why aren't you laughing?" Sabah asked.

"I don't like blasphemy."

Sabah hit the back of Amel's neck as a doctor would a newborn's bottom. "Laugh, I tell you. Laugh!"

Amel would not. Sabah was aware of his religious beliefs and should respect them. It was no secret that Amel, at seven years old and having grown up to be the most serious and obedient child in the neighborhood, thought he was good enough for employment in the House of God. Yet, as good a boy as he was told he was and knew himself to be, the older he grew, the harder he strove toward righteousness, never lying, cheating on tests or pestering girls. He accumulated good deeds like Coke caps with prizes at stake.

"Don't get on my nerves. Put yourself to use," he remembered his mother having said when he approached her with his plans.

Knowing he wouldn't get parental assistance, Amel took matters into his own hands. He convinced a friend to run away from home and enter the priesthood with him. He drew such colorful images of the place they were going, the friend thought they were joining the circus.

With no more than a dirham between them, they walked to the convent of the nuns who taught them catechism. When they told the nuns their intentions they were smiled upon, welcomed like kings, seated at tables and served more food than their mother gave them at Easter or Christmas. But when they finished eating, they were patted on the heads, told what nice little boys they were and gently told to go home before their mothers got worried.

"Why weren't we allowed to stay?" Amel's friend asked on their walk home.

"You disqualified us."

"I did not."

"You did so."

"When?"

"When you stole the neighbor's pigeons."

"That was a week ago!"

Amel shook his head. "I told you to stop tricking them with those fake bird noises, and you wouldn't listen."

"That was a week ago!"

"You didn't even have enough room or food for them."

"Yeah, but that was a week ago!"

"God's memory goes back months." Amel stopped and kicked some sand. "It's all over. They'll never take us."

"Good," his friend kicked sand too. "Those nuns give me the creeps. They dress like witches." And he walked on in a hurry.

Amel was not happy he had failed, but when he got home that night he kept up his devotions. He wore white pajamas, put a rosary around his neck, held a wooden cross in front of his chest and told his younger sister, who was laughing at him, to take his picture.

His mother also laughed. "What are you doing?"

He didn't answer. The convent might have rejected him, he thought to himself, but he wouldn't let that discourage him from being a priest when he grew up.

"Are you going to drink your Pepsi?" Sabah asked.

"I've been drinking it."

"I mean, do you plan on finishing it?"

Amel handed him the half-empty can.

"That's too bad about your rejection," Sabah said, shaking his head and gulping the drink. "Talaal Sitto was granted a visa, so was Najah Aqroui, Salam Ouro, Moneer Brikho." He burped and rubbed his flat stomach. "I hear the story you give them means zilch. See, each morning the immigration officers meet before the embassy opens. They say 'Today, we'll give five visas. Two to Iraqi single women, two to Iraqi families, one to an Iraqi single man.'"

Amel sighed in exasperation.

"What are you worried about, anyway?" Sabah asked. "You have wealthy aunts and uncles in America who'd send a private plane for you. I'm the one who'll amount to nothing but a street sweeper."

"Sabah, please shut up. I have things aside from the visa to think about."

"Like what?" Sabah asked, excited.

"My mother's niece, Dunia, is coming to visit from America and my mother expects me to host her and show her around."

"Why is she coming?"

"She's taking college courses in Athens."

"Did your Aunt Wafaá send her to marry you?"

"If Aunt Wafaá wanted me to come to America in this way, she would've come up with a dozen girls," Amel said defensively. "But neither she nor my uncles want me to resort to marriage as a means to reach America. They have higher goals for me."

Amel recalled Aunt Wafaá's kindness. She lived in Michigan and while visiting Baghdad years ago, she bought them expensive gifts like video games and roller blades. She also promised his family a mansion and a choice of businesses in America.

"Uncle Jabir already has one of his seven stores in my name," Amel said.

"Really?"

"That's right, I'm his business partner." Amel crumbled his lunch bag, threw it on the street and watched it blow away with other garbage beneath a trolley. "That's why I'm so mad. Here, I'm working as a furniture builder and deliveryman. I'm going to wind up with a crooked back if I keep carrying dressers and couches up and down stairs."

"I bet Wafaá is going to send at least two, three hundred dollars with your cousin," Sabah said in a daze. "Your cousin might give you a hundred or so too. Add them up and you're set for the winter."

That idea made Amel happy, until he caught himself. "I don't care about money."

Lunch break was over and the men returned to work. As he was working, Amel stressed out over his cousin's arrival. She would expect to be taken to dinner and shown around. He didn't have time or money or his own place. He lived with a paternal cousin, Shams, her husband and their seven children to save on rent and food but mostly, to make his family happy. They figured sharing a house with a family would keep him out of trouble.

But he was fed up with this arrangement. His cousin took three quarters of his pay, served him leftovers and complained about his slacks and sweaters taking up room on the clothesline. What about her husband's size 52 pants?

"Demitri," his boss called, "start painting the chair. Remember, peach and mint green."

Biting his lower lip, Amel went to grab the cans of paint. His boss was a nice man, but too philosophical. Maybe it was the Greek genes. Just because he owned a lot of lumber, he talked about trees like they were women. "You don't see it, Demitri, but each season bark curves softly over bark. That's how a tree thickens. Each of these flowing lines—" He pointed at a board, "—is one year of a tree's life."

What did wood have to do with anything? Amel wanted to ask him. One couldn't eat it, or wear it. His boss should take more interest in money and pay his employees double. The drachmas Amel earned for his slaving allowed for two treats a week: a souvlaki sandwich and McDonald's.

The rest he saved for emergencies like his first days in Athens when he had to reuse chicken bones to make broth. During that time his mother had called to inform him she was holding a party in his honor, serving guests lamb, cake and cola. Cakes and colas were forbidden after the war due to their high sugar content, yet she had obtained them through the black market. He had thanked his mother profusely, then had gone to bed on an empty stomach.

Dipping the brush into the peach paint, Amel suddenly realized the irony of a cash gift from Dunia. It would be spent on hosting her. Since she was staying for months, she would strip him of the drachmas he had hidden in his closet, next to his identification papers and family pictures. He would have to be sure not to take her anywhere there was an entrance fee, and under no circumstances would he take her to McDonald's—only fast food restaurants.

CHAPTER 2

In the evening, Amel and two others were sent to deliver a bedroom set. The building didn't have an elevator and the apartment was on the third floor, with narrow stairways. Two and a half hours were spent carrying the dresser inside. The old woman gave them a good tip, but Amel's shoulders ached badly.

Sitting in the bus on the way home, Amel stared out the window at the crowd. People's problems were never the same, he thought. Furniture buyers worry if they've chosen the right color, fabric, design. They fret over cracks, prices. He, builder and carrier of tables and chairs, wiped sweat off his brow, sawdust from his mouth and clothes, returned home—sometimes to only a cucumber for dinner—slept with muscles burning, head hurting—then woke up to build a cabinet.

Earlier at work, his Uncle Jabir called from Arizona to give him strength and courage, yet Amel was solemn as he stepped off the bus. His cousin awaited him with a piqued expression. His visa rejection undoubtedly solidified her hatred for him. She probably thought she was stuck with him forever. Amel was sure she had taken him in only because she expected to get something out of his uncles in America.

Shams didn't serve him a crumb. From the look of the garbage bag he knew they had had boiled eggs and potatoes. He smelled pickled mangos too. He opened the refrigerator and felt her head turn. His nostrils flared. She didn't even have the decency to be out of sight. He decided to provoke her. Sabah had suggested they live together. His house down the street was large and cheap because like beets and carrots, nine tenths of it was underground: damp, dark and cold.

Eager for her to kick him out, he deliberately kept the refrigerator door open.

"What, you're letting in fresh air?" Shams asked. "You think this is a window?"

It worked. He ignored her and she accused him of extravagance.

"Don't worry," he said. "I'll reimburse you for the bread you feed me."

"Oh, so now I'm starving you, am I? Of course, how could you know my struggles? You're not the one with eight mouths to feed...."

He didn't hear the rest because he was correcting her in his head; as big as her husband was, and as monstrous as her children were, she had sixteen mouths herself. He had to say something. "If I didn't know your struggles, I wouldn't have kept my mouth shut for as long as I have."

One by one, members of the household came to watch the drama. Popcorn, tea anyone? Amel asked silently. Sabah then knocked at their door. He asked why Shams was shouting.

"He's an ungrateful, insensitive punk," she said to Sabah.

Sabah took Amel's side, which put Shams in a frenzy.

"Look who I'm talking to. You want Amel as a roommate so you'll...." She slurped the palm of her hand, "...all his money."

"Me?" Sabah cried. "I care about Amel so much, I'm willing to give him the shirt off my back."

"We'll see who'll give what to whom."

"Why are you attacking him?" Amel asked. "He hasn't done anything to you."

Shams marched towards the front door and opened it. "Go," she said, extending her arms out. "Enjoy Sabah's generosity."

A few more words back and forth and both men were booted out. Sabah helped Amel move his things to his house. They sat on the couch, Sabah happily reenacting what happened at Shams' house.

"I swear, had she said another word," Sabah said, punching his left palm, "I would've—I would've—I don't know what I would've done."

"Yeah," Amel sighed, sadly.

Sabah slapped Amel's thigh. "Cheer up, Cousin. I'll make hamburgers and tea, we'll watch TV and in comparison to where you were, you'll think you're on vacation."

A week later, Shams sent her youngest daughter with a message. "Your cousin Dunia called," she said, handing him a paper. "Here's her number."

Amel didn't have a phone, so he grudgingly went to a kiosk to call. Dunia's greeting was in perfect Arabic but brief, businesslike. Right away she mentioned the items and cash Wafaá had sent him and asked when he would pick them up.

"I work late every day," he made it clear from the start. "I can't see you until ten tomorrow night."

She agreed and gave him the address of her hotel. He wrote it next to her phone number, then lost the paper. The next night, with Sabah beside him, they went from place to place asking for directions. Luckily he remembered the name of the hotel and that it was near Omonia Square. By ten thirty they found it. He called her room then sat with Sabah in the lobby.

Five minutes later he saw her come down. She was tall with a skinny face, long nose and bright eyes. Her layered hair reached down to her tailbone. She was dressed in black stretch pants, a white sweater and flat sandals. The top of her sweater slipped slightly off one shoulder.

Amel melted like an ice cream cone in the desert. His memory crowded his swollen mind as he traveled two years back to when he was seventeen and his Aunt Moneera visited Baghdad. She gave his mother a wallet size of her oldest daughter's senior picture. One look at the girl wearing white cap and gown, holding a diploma, smiling assuredly, staring intelligently, as though she had read all the books on the shelves behind her, and he experienced first love. He read the back of the picture—a few words written to her aunt, then the signature, Mona.

Astonished, he couldn't have stood up to shake hands had Sabah not pushed him. She approached Amel first and shook his hand. "Hi," she said, then sat beside him.

It was the shortest greeting he'd ever encountered. At the sight of a relative, people generally express joy, give compliments, ask about the family's welfare, give regards from so and so, then sit down and repeat the process.

"We're late because I forgot the address at home," Amel said, then explained in detail their half hour of searching.

"Good thing you found me," she said. "I wouldn't have called again."

"Why not?"

"The woman who answered the phone was rude."

He was concerned. "What did she say to you?"

"I asked if I could speak to you, she said you weren't there. I asked to leave a message, she said, 'I don't know if I'll see him again. What do you want?' I told her I was your cousin from America and she suddenly turned nice."

Amel and Sabah looked knowingly at each other.

"Who is she?" she asked.

"She's my father's first cousin," Amel said. "I was living with her until we had a fight. Then I moved in with Sabah." He eyed Sabah. "Because he took me in, she's upset at him too."

"You're lucky she gave you my message."

"She knew better than not to," he said. "So you saw my Aunt Wafaá before you came?"

"She sent things for you. She said to tell you to be strong and not to worry while she and your uncles find a way to get you out."

Saddened, he nodded.

"Do you have a new number then?" she asked.

"We don't have a phone," Sabah said. He turned to Amel. "Give her your work number."

"You know, I was expecting someone else to show up," Amel said, searching his pockets for a pen and paper. "You once sent us a picture of you, signed Mona."

She laughed. "That's Uncle Salwan's daughter. I can't write Arabic. My mom was busy packing. So Cousin Mona addressed my senior pictures to relatives. She mistakenly signed her name."

Amel was speechless.

"What's the matter?" Dunia asked.

"Nothing. When did you arrive?"

"Four days ago."

"Who brought you here?"

"Actually, this isn't where I stayed the first night. I stayed at a hotel near the airport but later thought it better to stay closer to downtown."

"You moved around all by yourself?"

"Hardly," she laughed. "A taxi drove me."

"Have you toured Athens yet?"

"I've walked around Omonia Square during the day."

"Omonia is different at night. You want to see? I'll buy you dinner too."

"It's eleven o'clock."

"So what? We eat as late as one, two in the morning."

They took the bus, her first time riding one. Amel couldn't believe it. She explained that in Michigan, where the three big American car companies were, everyone drove. Her first taxi ride had been to the hotel from Anatoliko Airport.

Amel bought Metro and trolley tickets, so she could get a bigger taste of public transportation. She begged him not to bother but he insisted, "In the name of obeying my mother's order to show my aunt's daughter around, I must show you around."

Through the noise of the roaring engine, spinning wheels and squeaky brakes, the loud driver and louder passengers, they became acquainted. At twenty-one, his cousin was sixteen months his senior, born and raised in Michigan.

Her parents taught her Arabic because it was a more worldly language. Still, she understood some Chaldean.

She was a junior at a university, majoring in history. After graduation, she planned to enter law school and eventually practice international law. Studying in Europe seemed like a good way to combine education and experience.

"Athens was actually last on my list," she said. "My parents consented to my studying abroad only if I picked a country where I have relatives. There was a thirty-eight-year-old male cousin living in Paris, and there was you." She laughed to herself. "The French option was rejected, you can imagine why."

Amel's turn came. He had to prepare, however, because her issues, compared to his, were biscuits. Carefully, he trod into his melancholy muddle. As he spoke, he tried to avoid sounding pathetic. Yet he could tell from the emotions in her eyes that it came out sounding full of self-pity. Sabah then tried to recite his trials, but no one cared to listen. Instead Amel suggested they go to a nice restaurant. His cousin swore she was not hungry, but he insisted. When they got there, she looked startled. "No, not here," she said.

"Why? It's delicious. They have great hamburgers called Bic Mags. Their potatoes are excellent too."

She shook her head. "It's too heavy this late at night."

He was quiet, pondering how to please her.

"If you want to buy me food, buy souvlaki. I don't know what it is exactly, but I've heard of it."

"Souvlaki? That's easy. But I wanted to take you someplace special."

"I'd prefer ethnic food."

"In that case I'll get you the best souvlaki in town," he said, hastening his pace. "There's a place near my house."

"That's far," Sabah complained.

"So what?" Amel snapped.

To get there, they took a bus, then walked one block. They bought souvlaki and sat on a curb. She ate; he watched her eat. She leaned over, her hair waving like a hazel flag, partially covering her sandwich, and brushing against his right thigh. Her hair didn't have a unique fragrance or feel like silk. Actually it resembled wool. Yet its uneven tousled strands intoxicated him.

She focused hard on her eating, licking sauce off her lips, oil drips from her hand. She pushed back her hair with her sleeve. As she finished the last bite, she willfully glanced at him. He felt with his heart they were about to start a love affair.

"Come with me." Amel helped her up and led her to a kiosk. Sabah tagged behind. "I'm going to call my mother. I want you to talk...."

"Amel, no," she said. "I wouldn't know what to say. We've never spoken before."

"So what? You and I had never spoken and here we are." Listening for a phone ring, he added, "Don't worry. There's only three thousand drachmas on this card. The line should cut off within five minutes." He hung up the receiver. "Let's hope we can reach her first."

After several attempts, he got through. "*Youm,* your niece arrived. Like I promised you, I'll take good care of her and show her around whenever she pleases."

"I'm glad you came to your senses," his mother said.

Excited, he babbled the rest of the conversation then gave the phone to Dunia. A few minutes later, he said into her left ear, "Tell my mom to hurry. The meter is almost at three thousand."

The line died, anyway, and she hung up.

"Was that so bad?" he asked, softly.

Their eyes locked together, like ten bananas hanging from one stem. Embarrassed, she soon turned her head. "Where's Sabah?"

"He went to peek at the nude posters."

They dropped Dunia off at two o'clock. Amel had the next day off and invited her to lunch at his house. He said he would pick her up at noon. "What's your favorite food?" he asked.

"Potatoes."

"Then I'll cook a potato casserole."

"Your cousin is pretty," Sabah said to Amel on their way home."

"Shut up."

"What—she's not pretty?"

"She is, but it's none of your business."

"It's strange how she didn't even kiss you. You're her first cousin, you haven't seen her in years, and she shakes your hand like you're a toothbrush."

"Be quiet. How do you expect her to kiss me, a man, a complete stranger?"

"You're not a man, you're her cousin."

"Shut up."

"Well, cousins kiss."

"Still. We'd never met before and she's a good girl. She's been raised properly."

"Your last cousin kissed you hello," Sabah pushed. "She wasn't good, I take it?"

"That was different. She was married."

Amel's bed swayed that autumn night, like someone had lifted it, placed it on a sea. The day he first saw Dunia's picture, he had had a serious talk with his mother. She was washing *burghul* in the sink when he announced, "I want to ask for my cousin's hand in marriage."

"Which cousin?" she asked, taken aback.

"Aunt Moneera's oldest daughter," he said with utmost formality: he didn't use the girl's first name.

She was quiet. She turned off the faucet and carried the bowl of *burghul* to the table. "She is not here that you can ask for her hand."

"Then I want her reserved for me. You must ask Aunt Moneera to give a word, a promise, anything."

"We'll see."

"If you don't tell her, I will."

She nodded in agreement and returned with an answer a few days later. "I discussed the matter with your aunt," she said. "We advise you to go to America first before talking further about it."

Amel was satisfied and considered his cousin now to be his fiancée. He took her picture and kept it in his wallet, showing it to everyone who crossed his path. He was almost giving them a wedding date.

That picture got lost on his way to Greece. But now Dunia had come to remove whatever in him had turned sour, old, cold. He lay in bed, knowing he was stepping into the unknown. But he knew it was beautiful.

CHAPTER 3

hile Sabah ate breakfast, Amel was out buying bread, beef and vegetables. He asked his neighbor Najieba for her best recipe.

"Good meal to choose for your cousin—inexpensive to buy and remarkably filling," she said laboriously. She was overweight, prone to agitation and five months pregnant with her fourth child.

She popped into his kitchen and was disappointed to see the potatoes' bare yellow flesh. She gave Amel a lecture. "Potatoes have lots of nutrients, but mostly in or just under the skin, which is high in fiber. Wash them well, but don't think water will remove any chemical residues. Be careful, Amel, not to store them longer than three months or soak them too long in cold water, or their Vitamin C will shrink in half."

Najieba inspected the red potatoes on the floor, which were oval and kidney shaped. "I prefer the brown round and long ones myself, but as long as they don't have a greenish tinge to the skins—which means they've been badly stored or exposed to light—they're fit to eat. Another thing—don't wash potatoes before storing, because that speeds decay. No one here can afford that, right?

"Brown paper bags are good for storing. Know that potato sprouts have poisons and should never be eaten. I'll teach you a trick. You can prevent old potatoes from blackening by adding a good squeeze of lemon juice or a teaspoon of vinegar to the cooking water."

"I'm making chili fry," he said, pouring oil into the skillet, so she'd get on with it. "Should I fry them with the beef and vegetables or separately?"

"One more thing, Amel, before I forget," she said. "Hold hot potatoes in a dish towel when you peel them so you don't burn your hands."

"Mom, *Babba* hit *Nunnu! Babba* hit *Nunnu!*"

Amel and Najieba looked up. Her two-year-old daughter pressed her face against the kitchen screen that connected to their back yard. "What happened?" Najieba asked.

"*Babba* hit *Nunnu! Babba* hit *Nunnu!*"

"Go inside! I'll be right there."

The child hopped away from the screen and ran. Amel told Najieba to check on her family, he would figure out how to cook the potatoes himself. She felt guilty about leaving him, but he encouraged her to go, knowing she'd already used her last breath lecturing him.

Five minutes later, Najieba's six-year-old daughter pressed her face against the screen. "My mother says to fry the meat and potatoes together, but the rest of the vegetables separately."

"Thank you, thank you. Now go home."

"Add a little curry to the potatoes—if you want—before you mix everything together."

He scratched his head. "I don't think we have curry."

Two minutes later, she brought him a teaspoon of curry. Amel cooked and quickly straightened the house before he and Sabah dressed to go meet his cousin. But Dunia wasn't in her room at noon. The receptionist said he'd seen her leave hours ago. By twelve-thirty, she still was not back. He got edgy, so Sabah told him the joke of the *Ourbi* and *Kurdi*.

"An *Ourbi* and a *Kurdi* were on an airplane. The *Ourbi* asked the stewardess if they have cream, and she said they do. 'Bring me cream then, since your face is like cream.' The stewardess smiled. The *Kurdi* thought he'd be cleverer than the *Ourbi*. So when the stewardess asked him what he wished to have, he said, 'Milk, since you are like a cow.'"

While Sabah chuckled, Amel kept his eyes on the glass door. Suddenly, he saw Dunia walk in with another man.

"Are you ready?" Amel asked, his blood boiling.

"Yes," she said breathlessly. She turned to the man and thanked him in English. He nodded politely and left. She then looked at Amel. "I went for a walk at 8:00 and got so carried away watching the vendors, shops, cafés and gypsies, I made too many wrong turns and couldn't find my way back. I asked one person after another for directions. Whichever way they pointed—north, south, west, east—I remained lost. I didn't realize so few Greeks spoke English. Finally, a clerk from another hotel had his bellboy escort me back."

He was so jealous, he took in her black shirt with an extra button left open, her short skirt of bright red and black. "Are you going to change first?"

"No," she said tersely.

He could have slapped Sabah rather than criticize her clothes, he thought. Yet he really didn't like what she had on. It wasn't in good taste to wear anything so revealing in the company of strange men. Last night's black stretch pants and white sweater suited her much better.

He worried how he would hide her from the leering men in the street. But as soon as she smiled at him, he relaxed, reminding himself that she was from America, not Iraq. For her, outfits that covered more than a bikini were modest.

This made him wonder. How would she regard his place, accustomed as she was to scholarly homes with modern appliances? His toilet didn't even have a seat. The house walls were made of green beans; a urinator's stream could be heard to the final drop, a groomer's teeth brushing to the last gargle and spit. His washroom was used for shaving, showering, washing and hanging personal laundry. Inside was a footstool to sit on, a tin bucket for retaining water and a plastic bowl for douching, an egg-shaped cracked mirror over the sink, a laundry tub in the corner, and a rope stretching from nail to nail. The kitchen had a full-size refrigerator and two burners, but no stove. In the adjacent hallway was a table with two chairs for eating. The rest of the furniture was half decent, considering it had come from people's garbage.

Other than that, his house was not so bad. There were no odds or ends to straighten up, only grease and dust to be swabbed. Spider webs, dead flies and cockroaches needed removal too.

"I love the way the balconies in Athens are filled with plants and flowers," Dunia said, observing the apartment complexes around his neighborhood. "Do you have a balcony, Amel?"

"Yeah, it's these flaps here," Sabah said, reaching for Amel's ears. Amel jerked away.

When they arrived Amel didn't detect disgust on Dunia's face. Either she wasn't shocked or she hid it well.

Amel placed the skillet on the living room table and passed around the bread. He offered Dunia a Pepsi, but she wanted tea so he put the kettle on. They began to eat. Once she finished her cup of tea, Dunia said she was tired and took a nap on his bed.

Najieba stopped by to see her, but since Dunia was asleep, she waited as Amel served her tea and biscuits. Eventually Dunia came out of her slumber, her eyes half-shut. She was introduced to Najieba, who was soon called over the kitchen screen to tend to a crisis at home. Dunia told Amel she was ready to return to her hotel. He and Sabah took her back.

"I'll check on you tomorrow after work," Amel said when they were in the hotel lobby. "I get off late, so I'll try to...."

"You don't have to," she interrupted. "I'll be fine."

"I might not be able to, anyway," he managed to pretend. "But I'll try."

Amel couldn't sleep. Traces of Dunia were all over his bed. The floral and ripe fruit fragrance of her body and the long hairs ascending like caterpillars on his pillow mesmerized him. There was even a tiny streak of lipstick on the tip of his sheets.

At work, he was in a livelier mood but he couldn't concentrate. He tried to remember his boss's tree philosophy in order to create a bond between him and the wood. All he could recall was that the wood of black ash trees was reddish and that of white ash trees blondish, sort of sandy. Both were stronger, more expensive, and recently, more scarce than pine and poplar wood.

He set down the glue on a desktop and walked over to his boss. "Sir, would it be possible to leave early today?"

Slowly, his boss picked wax out of his right ear and flung it on the floor. "Demitri, I have—you know how many orders to be delivered? An entertainment center, one. A baby room, two. Bar stools, three. A book shelf, four."

Amel returned to the desk he was working on. A little later Sabah approached him. "What did you ask?"

"Nothing," Amel said.

"To leave work early?"

Amel didn't answer.

"What did you want to do that for? You get paid by the hour, remember?" Amel lowered his head. "How much did Wafaá send you, by the way?"

"Two hundred dollars."

"What about Dunia's mother? Did she send anything?"

"A hundred dollars."

"Wafaá should've sent you double what she did."

"She would, if I'd let her. But I don't want unnecessary help from my father's siblings. They've done plenty for me already, and when the time comes, they'll do plenty more."

"What will you do with the three hundred dollars?"

"Save them, what else?"

"You want to buy a stereo?"

Amel bit his lower lip. "Sabah, if we weren't in public, I'd take this desk and glue it to your head."

He left work at 11:50 pm and rushed to catch a bus. The buses stopped running at midnight and taxis charged double. He made it to her hotel at 12:10 and called her room.

"Are you alone?" she asked.

"Yes."

"Then come upstairs."

He took the elevator to the sixth floor. Her door wasn't closed, so he knocked lightly as he pushed it open. She sat Indian style at the head of her unmade bed, her face free of makeup and hair flowing over her arms. She had on ankle socks and a short, ruffled beige nightgown that revealed her striped panties and soft nipples.

Amel quietly sat in a chair opposite the bed.

"I spent most of today alone," she said. "I walked, window shopped, slept, watched television. By midnight, I wasn't tired and didn't know how to pass the rest of the night. I was saved by your phone call."

He didn't know what to say.

Like a cobra, her body flexed towards the end of the bed. With her forehead pressed against the mattress, he saw only half of her. "I feel trapped in this room," she said. "There's so much I could see and do but my classes don't start until next week. I can't speak the language, I know no one."

"I could try taking a few days off of work...."

She lifted her head. "It's not that! Oh everything's a mess. I haven't a permanent place to stay. I'm supposed to have an apartment by now."

"What apartment? Aren't you staying in a dorm?"

"Never mind." She dropped her head again and rested it a while before looking up at him. "This isn't what I expected. Some stupid woman—a friend of my mom's—said there were furnished apartments for rent everywhere, she refers me to this one guy and he says the exact opposite."

"Why don't you stay at my place?"

She looked at him in bewilderment.

"I wanted to ask you that from the start," he said, "but I wasn't sure you'd feel comfortable—because of Sabah. But we work together all day so no one will be in the house to bother you."

He gave her a chance to respond, but she kept still.

"It's better than here, Dunia. My neighbors can show you around or get you what you need. There's Najieba and her family and there's another married couple with three daughters. They're all good company too."

She kept staring at him with the same expression until the phone rang. She picked up and after listening to the caller, fumbled over her words. "Yes, okay. I will," she said uncomfortably.

When she hung up, there was a change of mood.

"It's the friend of my mother's friend," she said.

He was dead quiet, feeling that they had disconnected from a minute ago. "I have no authority over you, Dunia," he said. "If you want to come to my house, it's your choice. If you want to stay here, you are your own person. Do as you like."

There was a moment of silence.

"I'll come to your house," she said submissively.

He was so pleased, the room lit up. They returned to treating each other like family as she shoved the clothes she had taken out of her suitcases back into them.

As they walked side-by-side into the street, Amel's happiness expanded through his cheeks and chest, like a tree during seasonal shifts.

"In spring, snap!" his boss once said, jerking his arms wide open, his belly forward. "Sap shoots up and wood fibers protract, because sap is a fluid, like blood and water, and can't be compressed. In autumn, sap pushes down so wood fibers have to contract, and you hear a cracking sound."

Maybe his boss knew something, Amel thought.

He put a cot for her in the living room and said good night. He slept uncomfortably, hoping the cot's wires wouldn't poke through the thin mattress, or the flat pillow and blanket weren't too flimsy against the night. He had a small heater, but it was dangerous to keep it on overnight. As his eyes shut, he felt a little guilty for having made her abandon lavishness for squalor. He didn't even have hot water. In order to wash, water was boiled in a pot, carried to the washroom and mixed with cold water.

But what could he do? He loved her and had to protect her.

CHAPTER 4

t five o'clock in the morning Amel woke up. He tried not to make noise, but the water pipes were loud and the walls thin. The loaf of bread he carved sounded like a saw against wood. He bagged his lunch and went to his room to get dressed.

He took his blanket and walked to the cot. He studied her, his mother's niece, his aunt's daughter, as she slept, eyelids like fresh bay leaf and lips like a clove of garlic. He covered her with his blanket, tucking it neatly beneath her chin. Before he left, he took one last look at her, then placed a spare house key on the table.

At work, his Aunt Wafaá called from Michigan. She and her brothers had heard the embassy in Rome was granting visas. "Aunt, you honestly expect me to smuggle into another country and learn a new language?" he asked.

"*Habbibi, azzizi,* if you're accepted, you'll be out of there in a matter of months."

"If I'm denied, I'll go crazy. At least here I've made friends and I have a job."

"Australia is another place...."

"*Aama* Wafaá, no. I'm not leaving Athens— not like that. You either find a guaranteed route to America, or I stay here or return to Iraq."

She was quiet momentarily. "Has your cousin arrived?"

"Yes."

"Did she give you the things?"

"Yes, thank you."

"Listen *habbibi, azzizi, dallali,* I'm going to do my best, I promise you," she said. "Meanwhile, Amel, if you need anything—big or little—call me collect. I'm like your mother, you're like my son."

Touched by her affection, tears formed in Amel's eyes. He loved his paternal aunts and uncles and he couldn't wait to make it to America and show his appreciation for all they had done for him and his family. Thanks to them, when the war first broke out, his family, unlike most others in Baghdad, remained in good shape. They were sent money regularly from America. At an exchange rate of three hundred dinars to a dollar—multiplied by a thousand dollars—the Aboona family moved from middle-class to wealthy.

Because his father's siblings were generous to whoever asked for help, other relatives benefited as well. For instance, when his Aunt Wafaá visited Baghdad, she gave alms to the church, donations to hospitals, medicine, clothes, cosmetics, candy and money to friends, even strangers.

Then again, Amel thought, given their massive wealth, what they did was probably normal, not charitable. When his Uncle Jabir, for example, visited Athens a year ago, he bought three suitcases worth of souvenirs for loved ones and two of gifts for himself. He stayed in a five star hotel, ordered room service, tipped big, always used taxis and never complained that anything was expensive.

Riding the bus home, Amel felt ashamed that he had considered returning to Iraq when his relatives in America had spent six thousand dollars getting him out. He stared out the window and wondered why he had such resistance to this land.

The fumes, city lights and traffic could fool one into believing he was in Baghdad, Istanbul, Belgrade or any downtown. Cities meant nothing on a map. It was people who marked a country; the way cats did their owners.

In the beginning, Amel hated the Greeks. They weren't welcoming towards him, suspecting he might steal or cause trouble like the young Albanians and Iraqis that loitered around Omonia Square. Once he gained their trust, they were polite and offered assistance. What he loved best about them was their honesty. One morning a woman forgot her purse on the bus seat. She retrieved it later in the evening, when the bus made its route back. What he liked least were their liberal ways. Their girls dated at thirteen and their kiosks were decorated with pornography.

At home that night, Dunia was asleep on his bed. He changed in the living room, and then went to cook dinner. He was opening the refrigerator when he saw her standing at the kitchen entrance. "I thought you weren't coming back until nine or ten," she said drowsily.

"I told my boss a cousin is visiting from America. I must spend time with her."

"But I'm not here for only a day or two."

He put on an annoyed expression and pointed to the refrigerator. "What's this stupid thing you did?"

"I don't do stupid things," she said. "This morning, I had an egg sandwich and coffee for breakfast in a café. Then I walked for three hours. On the way back, I stopped at a supermarket. I bought cereal, milk, chicken and tea. Then I took a nap on your bed."

"I was going to shop tonight."

She headed towards the living room and he followed. "Tonight wouldn't have solved my morning's problem," she said. "You had no coffee and no tea."

"There's tea in the top left cupboard...."

"You're mistaken. There's no tea in this whole house. I checked."

He marched to the kitchen, returned with a dented rusty can, opened its lid and placed it under her nose. "Then what's this?"

She sniffed it. "I don't know. Hashish maybe."

"It's tea leaves!" Snubbing him, she turned to walk away, but he grabbed her arm. "I don't want you to go to the market," he said.

"Why?"

"I don't want you to get lost."

"I will go anywhere I please and I will get lost and find my way back however I want, and every day too."

He wanted to exhibit dominion over her but couldn't do it with words. She could outsmart him. So he stared into her eyes until her cheeks looked like red peppers. She tried nudging his hand away but didn't succeed.

"What?" she cried, as he pointedly pressed his insistence through his stillness.

Loud footsteps and giggles broke the spell. "Amel! Amel! Open the door," squeaky little girls' voices called. "Amel! Amel! Open the door."

Amel let them in. They were the neighbor's three daughters: Manal, Maysoon and Maram. They could've been mistaken for triplets had it not been for their different heights.

"Why are you bothering me?" Amel asked, playfully slapping the oldest's face.

The squeaks increased as Manal pushed his hand away. "Our parents want to meet your cousin. The one from America."

"What do you have to do with it?"

"Oh Amel, come on," her squeaks rose higher. "What should we tell them?"

"Get out of here," he said. "You're bothering me."

"Amel, this is not a joke." They peeked over his head and under his arms. "Is that her?" Maram, the youngest, asked.

"Hey, it's not your business," he said and pulled Maysoon's hair. "Go tell your parents to come over for tea tonight."

"Okay, mister."

"And you better not come with them," he shouted as they ran back to their home, a few steps away.

"Oh yeah? Really Amel, like we'll listen to you," they giggled.

Amel told Dunia he didn't want to eat in and took her out for souvlaki. When they came back, Sabah was home watching television. "Where were you guys?" he asked.

"We had dinner," Amel said.

"And didn't bother to bring me anything?"

"Why should I bring you anything?"

"There's chicken in the freezer," Dunia said nicely. "It shouldn't take long to defrost."

"Don't be concerned about his stomach," Amel said. "Since we moved in together, he's done well for himself. 'I'm broke and tired,' he always says and makes me do the shopping, cooking and cleaning."

Dunia asked about the neighbors, in an attempt to keep Sabah and Amel from bickering.

But they weren't ready to harmonize. "They're decent people," Amel said curtly. "Anyway, you'll meet them yourself soon." The two men continued their squabble.

At ten o'clock, Hakeem and Kareema came over. Both tall, thin, blue eyed, dark haired and in their late thirties, they looked like brother and sister. They were kind, but like the rest of the Iraqi refugees, in trouble; they couldn't get jobs or register their children in school; they had one room with a couch and bed, used Najieba's kitchen and toilet, and their sink was their douche. And they didn't have relatives in America to petition for them.

"Except for my wife's uncle," Hakeem sneered, "who has as much money as India has curry. This man condemned us for fleeing Iraq. Why? So he wouldn't be obligated for our expenses. What sort of uncle avoids his niece and her family's hunger? What human being allows his brother's daughter to resort to strangers—yes, strangers—for money? Does his species actually exist in America? Have you seen the likes of it or is only her uncle that despicable?"

"You asked him for help, directly, and he turned you down?" Dunia asked.

Hakeem laughed in sarcasm as he turned to Kareema. "Tell her, wife."

"I've written him several letters describing our situation," Kareema said softly. "I've even sent pictures. But he never responds."

"He doesn't care!" Hakeem roared. "The bottoms of my sandals have more feelings than this rock who without any shame calls himself an uncle. A human who doesn't care is what? A cardboard box. A killer."

"Relax your nerves, Abu-Manal," Amel told him, smirking. "It's not worth it to get upset like this."

"It's not that I'm upset. But I want to know...." He looked at Dunia. "Please make me understand, how does a human have intestines, lungs, liver, kidneys, and not feel a damn thing when his niece says, 'Uncle, my kids have only crumbs to eat'?"

"You forgot the heart, Hakeem," Amel teased.

Hakeem raised his left brow. "Heart? Heart, you say? That, *akhouya*, was left on the surgical table the last time the doctors opened him up. That's how he could be okay with his great-nieces dressing in scraps, living in a hole like mice, losing years of education and family relations, stranded in Greece."

"Wouldn't it be easier to settle here?" Dunia asked.

"I wish! This is a beautiful country if you're a citizen. Otherwise, you're a humiliation, a nobody. You can't get a job or attend school. And that pig— that inhuman uncle who thinks we're here having fun—let him come and see us one day. Our condition will make the heart he left on the table jump right back in his chest, and he will feel."

After the neighbors left, Amel told Dunia why Hakeem was so angry. He had never been accepted by Kareema's family, who were wealthy enough to have maids, cooks, chauffeurs and tutors for their children. Their couches and tables had patterns engraved in gold. They had suitors of doctors, lawyers, engineers, and pilots lined up for their daughter. Still, she wanted the electrical repairman who didn't even own a shop but worked for his brother-in-law. Her parents told her that Hakeem was after her money, that he was lazy.

"It's true, he is lazy," Amel said. "Here in Athens, with a family to support, Hakeem avoids finding a job."

Kareema didn't get her parents' blessings, so she ran away with Hakeem. They eloped and the family cut off all contact with them for three years. Then one day, a female relative who took pity on Kareema, having seen her constant sobbing, convinced them to at least allow her to visit. "Don't you want to meet your daughter's daughter?" she asked. "What fault is it of the child that she should grow up without maternal grandparents, aunts, uncles, cousins?"

Kareema's family agreed, on one condition: Hakeem would not show his face. Kareema accepted, which hurt Hakeem deeply. She explained to him that in time, whatever grudge they had towards him would be wiped out. For now, she herself couldn't wait any longer. Although eventually her family did speak to Hakeem, they kept their distance and if an opportunity arose to remind him how little they liked him, they took it. His decision to move his family overseas made them hate him. He had daughters, not sons—Iraq wasn't a threat to him.

"She doesn't look the type to run away for a man's sake," Dunia said.

"She did it for love."

"Maybe it's better if people didn't do things for love."

"You wouldn't drop everything for love?"

"No, I believe in logic."

"What do we care what people do?" he said, ignoring her remark and picking up the teacups and plate of cheap cookies. "We mind our own business."

Amel washed the dishes as Sabah changed into his pajamas and Dunia read.

"By the way," he said from across the house. "My Aunt Wafaá called at work today. She sends her regards."

"That's nice of her," Dunia said.

He joined her in the living room. "She's a nice lady."

She flipped a book page. "I don't know her well enough to say."

"You don't know my Aunt Wafaà?" he asked, surprised. "What about my Uncle Jabir?"

"No, him neither."

"My Uncle Jabir—in Arizona?"

She shook her head, her eyes on the book.

"Your mother knows them very well," he said. "My parents lived with them until they moved to America. You know, I would've been in America by now had it not been for my father. When he visited America during the Iraq/Iran war, he hated it so much, he refused to wait for his green card. He swore never to let his children go to America. Now he and my mom pray I make it to America."

She burst out laughing.

"What's so funny?" he asked, stunned. Within seconds her expression had gone from sympathetic to facetious.

She couldn't stop laughing long enough to explain. He waited as she coughed and tears rolled down her eyes. Covering her face, she said, "Oh, my God," several times, but could not utter another word. Finally, she took a deep breath.

"Dunia, what is it? Why did you laugh?"

"The way you said America a thousand times; to America, in America, above America, below America."

He stared at her so fiercely that if she had been any other person—or even an object—they or it would have moved. In her case, however, she sighed deeply while grinning at him. "You asked why I was laughing. I hope you didn't expect an untruth."

"Oh no," he said coolly. "Of course not."

"Good. I don't have a problem with lying, but I sense you're not one to fully comprehend its art."

He was so hypnotized by her confidence and gaiety, he couldn't move. He would never tire of watching her, but it wasn't up to him. She asked him to leave so she could change into her nightgown.

CHAPTER 5

veryday, Amel and Sabah left for work at 5:30 and came home between nine and eleven at night. Dunia's classes were starting in a few days so she began her mornings around ten. She took walks to her university, sat in cafés, came home for lunch then napped. In the evenings, she stopped at Hakeem and Kareema's for some philosophy, gossip and cocoa or coffee.

Often she took the girls and Najieba's youngest child to the kiosk and bought them treats. Amel asked why she didn't visit Najieba. Dunia said she didn't feel comfortable in her company. "She's very matter-of-fact," Dunia said. "Because I can't pay attention to some of what she says, she thinks I'm either an airhead or a brat."

Aside from that, she added, Najieba's husband, Ayad, was usually home by four o'clock. Dunia liked Ayad. He didn't say much and the way he minded his own business in the Iraqi refugee neighborhood of Akernoon impressed her.

Whenever Amel got off at his bus stop his heart pounded. Dunia was a block away, sitting on the neighbor's couch, waiting for him. He was anxious to see her yet wanted to prolong the anticipation.

He bought her a super-size chocolate bar with hazelnuts before reaching Kareema's door, and gave it to her during their short walk home. She thanked him profusely, unwrapped the candy eagerly but refused to share a single piece with him. Once home, Amel cooked dinner. Around midnight they set the table, and while Sabah ate quietly, Dunia and Amel argued. She declared his meals to be greasy and soggy.

"Vegetables and meat don't cook without oil," he said.

"Then how do you suppose potatoes are boiled?"

"That recipe is for something entirely different, Dunia," he said defensively. "Anyway, you shouldn't complain so much while eating. It's bad manners...."

"And another thing!" she interrupted. "Baked chicken shouldn't be fried first...."

"It has to be, so there's sauce to dip bread in."

"Two tablespoons of water would take care of that."

"No, it wouldn't. Poultry skin alone soaks up a cup of water."

One night he deep-fried *basterma* and *koufta* and she went ballistic, saying, "Ground beef has its own fat!"

Looking at the two inches of oil in the pan, Amel scratched his head in confusion. "Where did you learn that?"

"Amel, I'm no chef but the way my stomach turns at night, I know what you're feeding us is poisonous."

After dinner, Amel made tea and they played cards in the living room. They always bet food. "If you win," Amel said to Dunia, "I'll buy you ice cream."

"I don't want ice cream."

"Then what do you want?"

"A souvlaki sandwich with fries."

"Fine, a souvlaki sandwich."

"With fries," she stressed.

"And if I win, you buy me ice cream."

"No. If you win, you buy me ice cream."

"That's a great deal, Dunia," Sabah said.

Before going to bed, Amel asked her what she had done all day. She updated him, reciting Greek words and phrases. Surprised, he petted her head and called her his smart cousin. "Still, no matter what you pick up off the street or from television," he said, "you'll never know swear words."

"Who cares? I'm not majoring in vulgar language."

"What are you majoring in then?"

She lowered her eyes bashfully. "I'm not majoring in anything."

"Really? Then tell me the classes you'll be taking."

"I don't know their Arabic translation."

"Say them in English."

"You wouldn't understand."

"For your information, I know French too."

"*Arche'ologie et sociologie.*"

"Rekojie shoaly?" he asked. She laughed so hard, he got mad. "No wonder you don't want to eat oil. You're afraid it'll plug up your brain and make you...." He twisted his hand as if he was turning a knob.

"Don't call me stupid."

"I didn't call you that."

"Almost," she said, raising her chin high.

"If you hate being called stupid, you'd better spend more time studying and less time roaming the streets. And by the way, where do you go and who do you see out there?"

"It's none of your business."

He grabbed her by the hair. "What did you say?"

"Let me go."

"Tell me first what you said."

"I said don't call me stupid."

He released his grip. "That's what I thought you said."

Her boldness was like an orange, strengthening his heart and perfuming his atmosphere.

After living together for four days, Dunia remembered that she had forgotten to call her parents. She had promised them that she would do so every other day. So Amel took her to a telephone booth. While she spoke to her mother, he waited outside and watched a group of boys play soccer in a fenced field. She called him over when she was done and handed him the phone. "My mom wants to say hi."

He felt uncomfortable. The last time he spoke to Aunt Moneera was when she visited Baghdad and he had his mother ask for her daughter's hand in marriage. He hoped she had forgotten his adolescent behavior. Luckily, Aunt Moneera kept their conversation very brief. Her main concern was that he watch over Dunia and treat her as a sister. She gave him her blessings and they hung up.

On the way home, he noticed Dunia's mood had changed. She was quiet and distant, looking at him disagreeably. He figured she missed her family and tried to make her laugh, pointing out the drunk who was strolling and whistling Greek love songs, and mocking the pot-bellied man sitting on a bench eating sausage. She ignored him, finally cutting him off with the announcement that she wanted a place of her own.

"You're my first cousin, just like a brother to me and us living under one roof isn't considered wrong," she said. "But you seem to forget you have a roommate. What will people think or say? You should've thought of that beforehand, but what's done is done. Now I must move out."

Dumb struck by the sudden outburst; Amel took a minute to collect his thoughts.

"I don't want to stay in a dorm, though, or live with strangers."

"I'll talk to my boss first thing tomorrow," he said. "I'll take Friday off to look for a place."

"That won't do, Amel," she said and went on to explain he had been in the country a short while, had little information on furnished apartments or inexpensive hotels, no contacts outside of Iraqi refugees and no time to search and compare different prices and locations. And, she wasn't about to have him lose pay for her sake.

"Besides," she said. "I know someone better qualified—the man who called me the day you picked me up from the hotel. He has been living in Athens five years and has a list of apartments for me to choose from. He has his own car, his own business, so it's no trouble for him to close shop and drive me around."

"You're going back to him?" he asked incredulously.

"What are you talking about?" she demanded. "He's offering to assist me, not sleep with me."

His face paled in shock and her rage doubled. They had walked twenty minutes to the telephone booth, but she wanted to ride the bus back. She stormed towards the bus stop, speeding up anytime he came near her.

They didn't speak to each other until bedtime. Afraid of agitating her, he had stayed clear of her path. By then the fury that had bubbled under Dunia's soft, child-like skin had dissipated. She slipped timidly into his room and asked if she could have a word with him. She sat on the rug beside his bed. "I don't want to go see that man without your permission," she said.

He didn't reply, and she rested her head on his mattress. Half an hour later, he patted her hair and told her to go to bed or else she would have neck and back pains tomorrow. "Where's Sabah, by the way?" he asked.

"He hasn't come home yet."

"You might catch the flu or pneumonia sitting on the cold floor. Go to bed."

"Not unless you agree to let me see that man."

He didn't say yes or no, and she kept begging.

"Fine, go see him," he gave in at last. It was two in the morning. He pulled the blanket over his head. "Now go to bed."

She was quiet for a while then nudged his shoulders. "Are you sure you don't mind me going to see that man?"

He heard her but wouldn't respond.

"Amel, I know you're sleeping, but why don't you mind me going, if you don't mind me asking?"

She repeated this question as he drifted off to sleep. When he opened his eyes, her head was still on his mattress. "Dunia, go to bed."

But her sleep was deep and he was too exhausted to do anything about it. In the morning, the lights were off, Sabah's bed was untouched, and she was gone. She had moved into her cot during the night. He prepared lunch, changed and went to her.

"Don't go," he said pleadingly.

She struggled to open her eyes. "This is business, Amel."

"I could do it for you."

Groaning, she lifted the blanket over her nose. Her eyes didn't consent. He growled in frustration and banged the door shut on his way out. He couldn't think straight the whole day, which Sabah noticed and came to him with one of his jokes.

Amel said to leave him alone, or else he'd whack him on the head with the lamp he was painting.

Dunia told Amel to take her to a hotel that night, since finding an apartment might take a while. He asked what was the hurry. "We've already gone over this," she said, packing her luggage. "Please don't try to persuade me to stay or I'll go downtown myself."

"Dunia, has someone bothered you? Did Sabah say anything to upset you?"

"No. The fact of the matter is I have to leave with or without your help."

"Did your mother say?"

"No!"

"I have Sunday off and…."

"It has to be tonight."

"Don't be crazy, Dunia, it's just one more night."

"One night is nothing to you but it's something to me."

He left her alone as she finished packing.

"Well?" she asked when she was done. "Are you coming or aren't you?"

He got up from his seat. She tried to help him carry her luggage, but he wouldn't let her. He set the suitcases on the sidewalk, told her to keep an eye on them and went looking for a taxi. Their first stop was across from a small hotel. The driver said he would stop the meter while they checked inside. Amel expressed gratitude in Greek, then said to Dunia, "He's a good man."

Amel told the hotel owner he wanted a single room with a balcony. "Who is it for?" the man asked.

"My cousin."

"Where is she from?"

"America."

"Ah, America," the man smiled, lightly touching Dunia's cheeks. "I have something I think you'll like." Eyeing her up and down, he added, "Beautiful. You'll like."

Amel's nerves tangled like grapevines. He wanted to knock the guy's teeth out, but they were dentures. The receptionist took them upstairs. The room was very feminine with delicate furniture and soft peach and blue colors.

"I like it," Dunia said right away to Amel.

Amel told the lady they would think about it and hurried them out of there. In the car, he got into a conversation with the driver and ignored whatever Dunia said. "I liked that hotel, Amel. Where are we going now? Why didn't you take up that nice man's offer? Let's go back."

He would not say a word, and she would not keep her mouth shut. "That wasn't a decent hotel," he finally said.

"How do you know? You've never stayed in hotels. Just because an old man was a little on the friendly side didn't mean he was...."

"That's exactly what it means."

Still she kept arguing. He told her to be still so he could figure out where they should go.

"Where we should go is back to that hotel." Seeing he would not consent, she pointed out other hotels they passed on the street. He said they were in bad areas. "Even better," she said. "They'll be inexpensive."

"You don't know what you're talking about."

"I do, but you're so stubborn you won't listen."

He ignored her for the rest of the ride to the hotel Amalia, located on Amalia Avenue in Syntagma Square. Pressing Amel's arms, she gasped, "This will cost a fortune."

"The driver says it has excellent off-season rates."

The street was mostly banks and government buildings. This was not an owner-operated hotel. The employees wore blue uniforms and used computers. The lobby was as big as a house, had a chandelier the size of the sun, expensive furniture and, Dunia noticed, a wide elevator.

"The first hotel I stayed in had an elevator the size of a phone booth," she said. "To top it off, the bellboy expected me to tip him. For what? Taking up what little air and space the elevator had?"

They went to the reception desk. The rates were not much higher than the other hotels and Dunia bargained for a weekly rate and got an eight-hundred-drachma reduction a night. Amel gave his tentative approval but said they had to see the room first.

The room was on the fourth floor, with two beds, a western bathroom with strong running hot water, a twenty-inch color TV with fourteen channels, a large closet, a table and armchair by the window and a balcony.

"It's perfect, don't you think, Amel?" she asked, her face glowing like a red apple.

"I like it."

Once she checked in and the bellboy brought up her luggage, she threw herself on the bed.

"Are you happy now?" Amel asked.

"Of course. Who wouldn't be in a room like this? At least I'll have the privacy I didn't have with Sabah around. I hated it when he went to work after you did or came home earlier. He always did that, one day complaining of a headache, another of a stomachache." She knelt over the luggage, searching frantically.

"What are you looking for?" he asked.

"My favorite nightgown, which I didn't dare wear at your house because of your roommate. Personally, I don't know how you can stand him. I guess it's a cousin thing. I like my paternal cousins too, even though their mothers are wicked—except for Aunt Affaf. She isn't so bad, but she could be, I'm sure. My maternal cousins...." She stuck her tongue out.

Lying on the bed against the wall, both hands behind his head, Amel stared at her. A variety of colors glowed from her, predominantly hues of violet. Maybe it was her shirt or some trick of vision. Once his boss had said to him while pointing at a tree, "Those purple leaves are all colors but purple." He pointed at another tree. "Those pink leaves are all colors but pink." He inspected Amel closely. "Do you know what I mean? See, white is all color. Black is absence of color."

Maybe she was all color.

When Dunia looked up, she seemed startled by his expression. She turned to the clock. "It's almost midnight. You must leave to catch the last trolley."

"I'll take a taxi," he said.

She frowned. "That's not entirely up to you. I don't mean to be rude but you must leave. I have to undress and you can't be here to watch. I could change in the bathroom but I won't, because why should I?"

His gaze darkened. Glancing at her watch, she said, "Only a few minutes left to go."

He wouldn't budge, so she grabbed his arm and tried to pull him up. "Why are you so heavy?" she asked, failing to move him. "You're tiring me out. What a mean thing to do after all the hours I spent looking for a hotel."

When he got up of his own accord, she pushed him by the shoulders to the hallway. "Come on, *yella*, bye," she said. As she closed the door, he kept it open with his foot. She put more weight against the door but couldn't shut it. Suddenly he flung it open and she stumbled backwards.

"I could've gotten hurt." She checked her toes.

"I'm leaving work early tomorrow," he said. "I want you to be here by eight."

"What time are you going to be here?"

"I'm not sure—sometime between eight and nine."

"Then why do I have to be here by eight?"

"Because I might get here at that time."

"And if you don't? Then I'll be stuck in the room."

"Do some reading, or rest."

"I'm tired of reading and I don't need rest."

"It's not my problem what you do, as long as you're here by eight."

"No."

"Dunia, by eight." He told her to lock the door when she was alone, not to hang out in the lobby at night, not to befriend strangers or roam around the hallway or take the elevators to other floors, and if a problem came up, to go to the receptionist right away then call him at work.

She was rolling her eyes and making faces. When he finished, he pulled her hair and asked, "Did you hear me?"

Her head backwards, she saluted him. "Yes, Saddam."

After he ruffled her hair and left, Amel strutted out of the hotel. The National Garden was straight across from the hotel, fenced by high-level shrubs. Next to it was a kiosk and bus stop. The smell of roasted chestnuts, cigarette smoke and car exhaust mixed with fresh September wind, blew gently against him. Suddenly, he realized he wasn't forsaken. Athens was a friend he had been blind to. Although it hadn't been the gateway to America, it had brought him Dunia, his fiancée, his fate.

CHAPTER 6

ow quickly things change form, Amel thought, looking at the sawdust that was once solid wood. Last week, he had been a hard-working miser, a tightwad who readily accepted money gifts. He had lost respect and consideration for family relations, culture and heritage.

In Baghdad, although he didn't have a job, he held a position in society through his parents. His pockets were never short of *dirhams* and dinars. He and his siblings were permitted to take what they needed from the cookie jar when they ran out of money.

In Athens, however, the drachma and a visa replaced family affection. Talk of money and America was the food of refugee homes. Dunia's presence changed all that. By hearing her say that parsley made a good eyewash and fresh strawberry juice could be used to clean the skin, he was learning to see a rich world in the local produce market, not just in America.

Amel arrived at hotel Amalia at 7:40. He called Dunia's room but there was no answer. He sat in the lobby and watched TV. She showed up at 9:10 with a guilty expression.

"Have you had dinner yet?" he asked.

"No, I haven't."

"What do you want to eat?"

"I don't care, whatever you like."

"I never did take you to McDonald's."

"No, you didn't."

"You want to go tonight?"

"Yes."

They went upstairs so she could freshen up.

"I ran as quickly as I could, I swear," she said as she brushed her hair. "I should've taken the trolley but I felt my legs were faster. I said to myself, by the time I waited for the bus and it made all its stops, Amel would be long gone. And I didn't want to chance getting a citation for not carrying a ticket."

"How many times have I offered to get you a bus pass?"

"I walk more often than not."

"Then buy bus tickets from a kiosk."

"That's a waste of money. The truth is I like walking and can't give it up for the sake of being on time. It suits my pace better; I can be as fast or slow as I want. It's more exciting. I like crossing busy streets, getting a close look at the merchandise, passing through a crowd of gypsies, well-dressed women in high heels. I even like the hooting boys who say lovely things in Greek."

She paused and looked at him knowingly. Amel's jaws were tight, his forehead pulsing and his eyes burning. Laughing, she grabbed her key and ran out the door. He followed and saw her heading towards the staircase.

"No, we'll use the elevator," he said.

"I haven't the patience to stand still in a box."

"Dunia, please, let's go."

"You're lazy and stairs are good cardiovascular exercise. I'll give you an example...."

"Please, Dunia, I'm tired."

Lowering her eyes, she obeyed. In the street he placed his arm around her shoulders. She didn't comment or remove it, and he wondered if she even noticed. Back in the room they lay beside each other on the bed and watched TV. He told her to look for him the next morning, because he'd wave to her as his trolley passed beneath her balcony at 6:23.

"Amel, that's early," she cried. "It's my last morning to sleep in before classes start and you expect me to ruin it?"

He convinced her to do it.

She walked him to the bus stop before midnight. While she sat on the bench, he stood an inch away from her, listening to her hair flapping and taking in its aroma of fruit shampoo, dust and souvlaki. People shuffled towards the curb as the bus came, so Amel told her to return to the hotel.

"I will once you're gone," she said.

"No later than that."

She agreed but remained seated. He pushed through the crowd towards the back of the trolley and saw she was still there. She smiled and waved. He gestured for her to go back inside. She stayed in her spot as the trolley turned. The minute he got off, he rushed to a phone.

"You needn't have bothered calling," she said. "I can take care of myself."

"Be at the balcony at 6:23 tomorrow."

She sighed in exasperation.

"Dunia!"

She promised. The next morning at 6:10, in the middle of switching buses, he called to remind her. "I'll be looking for you, so be there," he threatened.

"I will, I will," she said.

She was nowhere in sight. Once he got off the bus, he told Sabah he would meet him at work in a few minutes, then fuming, marched to a phone.

"Hello," she said drowsily.

"Why weren't you on the balcony?" he asked.

"I was."

"You weren't. I passed by exactly when I said I would and you weren't there."

"Then you were looking at the wrong balcony."

"There was no one on any of the balconies."

"I stood there for twenty minutes."

"You didn't."

"Amel, why would I lie?"

"I have to go into the shop now," he said. "Don't come back late tonight."

"What's late?"

"Just be there before eight."

"I'll try."

"Dunia?"

He arrived at her hotel at 8:40, went straight to her room and knocked on the door. She opened it and said in a rush, "There's no time to eat or sit down. I have great news. I found an excellent apartment—not far from here, very cheap too. It doesn't have a phone, but that's okay. We're closing the deal in less than an hour."

"Who is?" he asked, baffled.

"The man and I."

"Which man?"

"It's too long and complicated to explain."

"When did all this happen?"

"Today."

He was quiet.

"Maybe we have a minute to grab a bite after all," she said. "If you're really hungry, which you probably are. Although we should get going."

"When did you see that man?" he asked.

"What man?"

"Whichever one you're talking about."

"The day I told you I would. But he's not the one who'll be there today. It'll be his brother, who knows the landlord."

"Why didn't you mention anything about it last night?"

She told him of the day's events, but he continued to be perturbed.

"What is it now?" she asked, impatiently.

He wouldn't speak. Looking at her watch, she begged him not to give her a hard time.

"Please Amel, be reasonable and let's go."

He wouldn't budge and remained too angry to speak.

"What did you expect me to do?" she asked. "If you wanted to be the one to find the apartment, tell me how you were going to do it. Your work schedule is in the way. You don't know any landlords."

"You don't have to know a landlord to get an apartment," he said. "The reason I didn't find you one is because no one offers leases for less than a year."

"I know, that's what I mean. This man knows someone who'll make an exception."

His face reddened. "If you found what you want, I don't see the purpose of me coming along."

"That's ludicrous. I want you to come with me."

"There's no reason to."

"There *is* a reason."

He looked at her with injured eyes.

"You're supposed to look after my affairs," she said. "I need you to be with me, to make sure I'm not cheated."

He was unhappy about going along, but went. They met the man, named Farook. He was in his thirties, short with curly hair and a round belly. His clothes didn't match and his briefcase was worn out.

Amel felt at ease. Dunia said earlier that Farook was married to a Greek woman and had attained citizenship through her, so he had travel and employment privileges and seemed settled. Amel had been suspicious of his intentions, but after seeing Farook's appearance, and having asked direct questions and gotten quick answers, Amel trusted him more.

"I convinced the young man to give her a six-month lease," Farook said, directing most of the talk to Amel. "But she has to pay two months rent in advance."

"That can't be possible," Amel said. "I've asked many people and was told in Greece, leases must run at least a year."

"True, but I know the landlord. I've explained the circumstances to Dunia. The man's father died last year and he and his mother are now running the business. He's young, kind and not very strict."

"But," Amel insisted, "from what I know, a tenant must occupy a space for at least a year. I've asked my boss and Greek co-workers. They all say the same."

"Would I have to sign papers?" Dunia asked Farook, interrupting the conversation. "What does that mean, anyway? Say if I broke the lease by going back to America before six months are up, could I legally be held accountable? What sort of measures could the landlord take against me? My credit wouldn't be affected, would it?"

"Once you're in America, you're in America," Farook said. "They wouldn't touch you because it'd be too costly. Don't worry about that. Leases are local procedures. They don't hold consequences for people who live thousands of miles away."

The landlord was friendly and accommodating. He told Dunia in English he wouldn't have required the two-months deposit in advance had it not been a short-term lease.

"Many Americans," he said, "not to say you, of course, come with the intention of staying six months, even longer. Then within two weeks, they pack their things and abandon the apartment. We landlords are left with losses and additional work. We must find another tenant. In the meantime, we make no profit."

Then in Greek he translated what he'd said to Amel. Dunia promised she wouldn't break her lease and run off; she was a college student and needed to finish her semester. She shook hands on the deal, and signed the papers Farook had read and approved. When it came to handing over the keys, the landlord said, "You must wait a few days. There are unfinished details in the apartment. I must also have your electricity, heat and water turned on."

They celebrated the night with souvlaki sandwiches, fries and peach juice up in her hotel room. She was so excited that she talked as she bit off chunks of food. "When can you take me shopping for a bed and pillows?" she asked. "I need a comforter too, sheets, a burner and a refrigerator."

"You don't need a refrigerator," he said. "Buy everything fresh. There's a store down the street and a fruit market on the other side of it. If you're low on something, I'll get it for you."

"Where would we eat? There's no carpet. We'll have to buy a table with four chairs."

"Why four?"

"In case we have guests."

"What guests? It'll only be me and you."

"Friends I'll meet at the university."

He looked at her in disbelief.

"What if Kareema's daughters came over?" she quickly changed the subject.

"Why should they do that? They have their own home."

"What if they invited themselves over?"

"No one invites themselves."

She looked at her sandwich and said airily, "Fine, two chairs and no guests."

They cuddled on the bed together. Suddenly, a flow of emotions overpowered him and he said, "I love you, Dunia."

She didn't respond. They stayed in each other's embrace in silence, then he kissed her shoulder. Soon after, she rolled off the bed and walked to the balcony.

"What are you doing?" he asked.

"It's 11:50, Amel. If you don't go now, you'll miss the bus."

"So what? I could always take a taxi."

"Paying five hundred drachmas for a few more minutes isn't worth it."

"Then I'll sleep here, on the extra bed. It's sitting here doing nothing, anyway."

"Impossible! How would you get ready for work in the morning without a toothbrush?"

"I'll use toothpaste alone."

"What would the maid think?"

"It's not the maid's business."

"I have class tomorrow. I need to prepare."

"What have I to do with that?"

She didn't try harder to convince him to leave. He was happy. Aside from being in her presence, the mattress, with its strength of brick and softness of bread, soothed his aching back. He hadn't had a decent night's sleep since he had left his mother's home.

"Well, at least take off your jacket," he heard her say. But he couldn't move. His eyelids closed easily as he slipped into another time and space.

CHAPTER 7

She was still sleeping when he left her room. He wondered if she would remember what he had said to her. He would not blame her if she didn't want to start a romance. He wasn't fancy like her. Her hairbrush alone, with its thick silhouette shape and pink flowers, intimidated him. He would be better off in America, but that was taken for granted.

And he was afraid of her layers and layers of knowledge. It was like pealing an onion without ever reaching the center. She knew that dandelion leaves could be used in salads and their petals made into wine. The only flowers he could name were roses and sunflowers. She talked of Pericles, how he ruled Athens long ago, helped it prosper, was the power behind its Golden Age, that he had ordered the construction of many temples, including the Parthenon.

"The who?" Amel asked.

"Parthenon! It's right on top of the Acropolis!"

"The what?"

One day she had asked if he knew that in 2600 B.C., people from the Middle East brought copper to Greece, and that Alexander the Great was planning to conquer Arabia when he got sick and died in Babylon? He dodged these questions by smirking. "I'd met Alexander once or twice," he said, curling his lower lip backwards. "But I didn't know that about him."

His Uncle Jabir called. He asked Amel several questions about his new living arrangements, work and money. Then he promised to get him out of Greece soon.

"America is worth having patience for," he said. "Once you're here, your sorrows will turn into riches. I have big plans for you, Amel, but there's no sense in giving details. I'm confident you'll soon see it in person."

Amel thanked his uncle profusely and told him not to worry. At first the visa rejection was like a tight rope around his neck. Now he was again grateful to God. "You've helped me a great deal, Uncle Jabir," he said. "When I get to America, I'll make it up to you. I'll return every dollar you've spent on me."

"I don't want anything from you but your happiness. You're like my son. All of us here love you as a son. We'll get you out of Greece, you'll see."

Dunia's presence and his uncle's encouragement eased the burden Amel carried. He zipped through the job, asked his boss if he could leave early, and got to Hotel Amalia by 7:30. Dunia showed up in the lobby twenty minutes later.

"I got off early," he said.

Smiling mischievously, she ran towards the stairs. He yelled at her to use the elevator but she was already gone. When he got to her room, she had locked the door. He banged on it, threatening to break it down. She dared him to try. He stood still to fool her into believing he'd left. In ten minutes the door squeaked open.

He jumped in front of her and, screaming, she attempted to close it again. He quickly pushed it open and wrestled her towards the bed. She tried to bite his hands. He lowered his mouth to hers and was just about to kiss her when the building began to shake. The room fell silent until Dunia asked, "What was that?"

"I don't know."

They stared at each other. Then they bounced up, rushed into the hallway and saw people leaving their rooms and going down stairways. They took the hotel key and followed them. It was an earthquake, the first one in years, people said. Outside, they looked up at her balcony.

"Imagine," Amel said. "What if the quake was stronger and the ceiling caved in and we died together?"

"Exactly," she said, the fear removed from her face. "That's why I don't want you to spend the night here. I don't want people thinking we're lovers because we're not and never will be. You're nearly two years younger than me. And anyway, I'm not interested."

"Really?" he said fiercely.

"Yes," she stammered. "The other reason you can't is because the management might kick you out, or charge me double for using the second bed. Also, I don't want your roommate thinking we have an intimate relationship. What if my family calls in the middle of the night and you answer by accident? You'll distract me from studying. Now that my classes have started."

"I'm going to drop you off," he said.

"You don't have to. I'm practically in the lobby. I'll be safe climbing the stairs. If it'll make you feel better, I'll use the elevator."

He was sad. She echoed his own concerns. He wasn't educated or stable enough for her. How could he compete with education and experience? She came from splendor; he was a product of harsh experiences. He stood there, glued to the spot.

"What now?" she cried in frustration.

"You don't even know what's bothering me," he said.

"Okay, what?"

"You hung up the phone on me this morning," he lied.

"What are you talking about?"

"You hung up on me before saying goodbye."

"That's the problem? I did say goodbye. And if that's what's bothering you, why didn't you say so from the start? Why drag it out until my throat hurts? Like the other day, you thought I wasn't at the balcony, but I was. We didn't see each other because there were five trolleys passing at the same time. What was the point of waving hello, anyway?"

His feelings hurt, he lowered his head.

"Enough," she said, fed up. "You have to go home now."

He consented unwillingly. At home, he couldn't sleep. She had hurt him, but she made sense. He hurried to the kiosk and called to apologize, but wasn't able to get through. The line was busy for half an hour, so he asked the receptionist to cut in.

"*Lipoume*," the receptionist said. "I'm unable to get through. She can't hear me."

"Try again, *parakalo*."

"I can't. There's a problem with the reception."

Enraged, Amel went home and told Sabah to get dressed.

"I can't get hold of Dunia and I have to make sure she's alright," he said.

In the hotel, Amel could hear Dunia from the hallway, laughing flirtatiously—his worst fears realized. He banged on the door.

"Who is it?" she called.

"It's me, Amel."

It took a while for her to answer. When she opened the door, she was in her beige nightgown and white socks, her hair a mess. She looked frightened. "What are you guys doing here?"

"Who were you talking to?" Amel asked.

Her face flushed in anger. "My brother."

"It didn't sound like your brother."

"How do you know?"

"Your line was busy for half an hour. Your calls to America last ten, fifteen minutes."

Her jaws tightened and her eyes narrowed. "Was this reason to hire a taxi and come banging on my door?"

"He got me out of bed," Sabah said. "We're lucky we found a taxi this late. But you should've seen how your cousin was on the way up here. The receptionist downstairs must've thought there was a fire chasing him from outside, and that your floor had a pool he could jump in."

Sabah checked out the hotel room. He tried to lift the television set. "Sons of dogs, they've bolted it to the counter," he said, then observed the phone. "Damn pigs, they've nailed it to the wall."

He went on like this, saying the owners were bastards for having such a heavy dresser. Good thing the pillows and blankets could be stolen. If the room wasn't on the fourth floor, he'd take the mattresses too. With the right truck and ladder, he might be able to.

Amel laughed at him. Dunia did too, but not for long. She reproached them both for coming. Sabah asked to be excused a minute. "I want a tour of the hotel because this might be the last time I see luxury," he said. "Besides, I could find furniture small enough to sneak out and take home."

When he left, Dunia confronted Amel, "Didn't you consider what Sabah would think before you dragged him all the way here?"

He bowed his head.

"Or was your jealousy the only thing working?"

She laughed sarcastically. "You put me in the most awkward position, Amel. And in front of who? Someone who I don't particularly trust and who had a grin on his face when he came into this room. He was well entertained and you're now at ease, I hope you both sleep better."

Sabah returned and complained of Amel's stupidity, which cost them a thousand drachmas each way for the taxi, to say nothing of the loss of sweet dreams.

"You guys go home now," she said, "or you won't be able to wake up for work tomorrow. I have classes too."

They left, Sabah excited as a child, Amel with a hunched back. Amel knew Dunia was going to add gray to his hair. Thanks to her intelligence he could end up looking like his father, who at fifty, resembled Santa Claus. He knew she hadn't been talking to her brother. But Amel's amateur way of handling the situation made him take back his accusations and plead guilty. He was at her mercy, like trees before a logger.

"Trees don't decide what they will be made into," he remembered his boss saying.

Feeling shame and defeat, he wished his boss was better informed about more important subjects, like Pericles, dandelions and anger, so Dunia wouldn't think Amel such an imbecile.

On his way to the bus stop the next morning, he called her from a kiosk. She didn't pick up, and he made several more attempts before he had to catch the bus. He used his lunch break calling her too, even though he knew she was in class. In the evening, he snuck away to a phone while their truck driver got gas. The receptionist said Dunia wasn't in her room and started to take a message when she stopped and called loudly, "Miss, you have a call. Pick up from next to the elevator, please."

"Hello," Dunia said in a huff.

"Why didn't you answer the phone this morning?"

"It didn't ring."

"I called you six times."

"I wasn't here."

"I called you before your classes."

"I left my room early."

"What are you going to do tonight?"

"What do you want?"

"Dunia, I asked you a question."

"I'm moving to the apartment."

"What time?"

She was silent.

"Dunia, when?"

"I don't know. Sometime in the evening."

"Wait until I get there before checking out. I'm leaving work at six."

She didn't say anything.

"You'd better wait Dunia, or else I swear to God...."

"I have to go," she said and hung up quickly.

When Amel got to her room, the luggage was stacked by the door.

"Should I take them downstairs?" he asked.

She refused to talk to him. Silently, they rode the elevator to the first floor. Dunia checked out, and they hailed a taxi. When they got in, Amel gave the driver his address. He told Dunia she would spend the night at his house.

"No, I want to stay in my apartment," she said. "I cleaned it today."

"Don't be crazy. You have no heat, no electricity, no furniture."

She insisted they go to her apartment, but he ignored her the rest of the ride. After dinner, taking no notice of him, she played cards with Sabah. Rather than hold a grudge, Amel gave her blankets, pillows and a coat the size of a sleeping bag for her apartment. Originally, he'd bought the coat for his sister in Baghdad, but figuring it'd cost twice its value to ship it, he'd kept it. He put the cot in the living room and went to bed.

They left together in the morning. He told her which bus and trolley to take from his house, and said he'd come over that night to check on her. "Don't bother," she said. "It's not necessary."

"I'll see you tonight," he repeated before leaving.

"Don't come!" she yelled after him. "Don't bother!"

He pretended not to hear her.

At 7:30, Amel asked his boss if he could leave work. "We have two deliveries today," he said. "I don't like it, Amel, that you're careless about your job lately. I understand your cousin is visiting from America, but should we close the shop on her account?"

Amel was so embarrassed he wanted to slap himself. To make things worse, the last order didn't go up the stairs smoothly. He wound up working until 11:30. His head hurt with worry about Dunia being alone in the dark and when he was done, he ran to the bus stop. He was looking out the window when he saw Dunia walking in the opposite direction. Shouting her name, he pressed the buzzer for the driver to stop.

He ran towards her, she towards him, until they locked in an embrace. He gave her a strong but brief hug because they needed to catch the bus before midnight. Leaning heavily against him and grabbing onto his jacket, however, Dunia weighed him down. In the bus, she sat so close to him he could barely turn his head.

"I was so frightened, Amel," she said, like a child. "When I finished cleaning, I read a little. Soon it got dark so I closed my books. I decided to go to sleep early and make a spot for myself in a corner. But the floor was cold. I started shivering."

"It's okay now," he said, kissing her head.

"I lay on top of the luggage, and when I heard something crackle, I got off. I told myself not to worry: Amel would show up soon, even though I told him not to. By 9:15, I wondered if my buzzer didn't work because the electricity was turned off. I thought you took me seriously and planned not to come."

"Didn't I tell you I'd come?" he asked.

"Yes, but I thought you wouldn't."

"Why wouldn't I if I said I would?"

"I don't know. I just thought you wouldn't come."

He stared at her tenderly. He loved her and knew she loved that about him.

"By ten I was scared and desperate," she said, looking away. "I wanted to go to your house but wasn't sure of the way. I hadn't paid attention when you gave me directions. I could find my way, probably, I told myself, but decided to wait for you. Your boss might have kept you late or you got stuck in traffic. Then my heart started beating very fast and my feet froze."

He explained why he was late then asked if she'd please not pull on his jacket because the zipper was gnawing at his neck. She slid her hand over his chest.

"At eleven I couldn't stand it anymore. I took my keys and purse and went outside. There were cats, at least ten of them, staring at me. Then I heard dogs howling. I thought the cats might attack and the dogs join in. I ran. I wasn't sure which way to go but I guessed and saw a main street. It was Amalia Avenue. I ran towards it like it was my mother. I was rushing to the bus stop when you called me."

He patted her arm. "Have you had dinner?"

"No. What's this?"

"What?"

She pressed. "This. What do you have under your shirt?"

"Nothing."

She opened his jacket and touched his chest with her fingertips. "Your chest is so hard it feels like metal," she said, then rested her head on his shoulders.

He was happy. Finally she found something she liked in him. She had almost paid him a compliment.

At his house, she followed his every step while he prepared dinner and sat close beside him while they ate. "You're not going back to the apartment until you have furniture, heat and electricity," he said.

"Okay," she said submissively. "Won't I need plates and utensils too?"

"I have extra in my cupboards."

"Okay. When can we buy furniture?"

"I'll take you to Monastiraki Sunday."

He made her wear his sweat suit to bed so she would be warm during the night and her clothes wouldn't wrinkle, and as she got ready for bed, she told him about an argument she had with the hotel manager. "I went to the front desk and asked why I was being charged an extra four thousand drachmas. I was told to talk to the manager. When I stormed into his office he said the additional fees were due to my having had a guest on two occasions. 'He's not my friend, he's my cousin,' I said. 'He's here to chaperone me until I move into an apartment, which happens to be today.'

'He doesn't have to stay inside the hotel to chaperone you.'

'Sir, this is a hotel,' I interrupted him, angrily. 'It is not a school. Then I walked out on him.'"

"Sorry you had to go through that for me."

"Oh, I was happy to put someone straight."

The next day he came home at seven, while Sabah went to a friend's. He changed into his pajamas and prepared hamburgers with eggs and potatoes while she sat in the bathroom, a tub of soapy water between her legs, washing her clothes by hand.

She yelled across the room that he'd better not fry the food with too much oil, and he called back that he was the cook, not her. "You don't even know how to hold a skillet. What did my poor Aunt Moneera bring into the world?"

"Do you think your mother did better having you?" she asked.

"Beauty, I must admit, her daughter has," he talked over her comments. "But that's all she has...."

"A hard head I must admit he has, but that's all he has...."

He left the food and went to the bathroom. Leaning against the door, he watched her quietly. Her straight back gently swinging to and fro, the tips of her hair in the tub, pants rolled above the knee, water splashing around her feet, she looked like one of the girls in Baghdad who helped their mothers with household chores. When she raised her arm to wipe hair and sweat from her face, she caught a glimpse of him and blushed.

"Come eat dinner," he said softly, and went away.

She abandoned the tub, and after dinner rinsed her clothes. She asked where to hang her undergarments so Sabah wouldn't see them. Amel made a curtain around the rope and said they should dry before Sabah returned. "He's going to the disco tonight and might not come back at all," he said.

Delighted by the news, Dunia ran to his room. "Since no roommate is coming tonight," she said, jumping into Amel's bed, "I get to have a decent sleep."

"What about me?"

"Sleep there." She pointed her eyes to Sabah's bed. "But turn off the lights first, and close the door behind you." He did so, but she continued, "Wait! Is the door locked?"

"Yes, it is."

"You'd better check."

"Forget about the damn door!" He walked towards her and got inside the covers.

"Go to your own bed," she said.

"This is my own bed."

"I'm not kidding, Amel," she said.

He hugged her, feeling the warmth beneath her damp clothes while inhaling the sweet smell of perspiration and laundry detergent.

"Get away from me," she said, flipping around like a fish just pulled from the sea. "You're suffocating me. I can't breathe. This bed is too small for both of us. I'm getting smashed against the wall. I'm choking. Get out. You're so annoying. Let me go. Move!"

But he persisted until he caught her.

CHAPTER 8

They kissed and made out with their clothes on. She asked him to buy her potato chips afterwards. "The green bag," she said, unable to translate sour cream and onion in Arabic.

He got her two bags. She finished one and saved the other. Wanting to read, she then kicked him out of the bed.

The kiss changed Amel's perception of the world. The Athenians, once crude people who growled if he browsed through a magazine in their newsstand were suddenly kind and flattering. They smiled upon him, even while spitting or urinating on street corners. The gypsies weren't the same, either. Their mud-honeyed hands and faces looked wholesome enough to lick. His boss, the tree lover, turned into a prince.

Amel was so elated that if someone had asked him his name, he would have only remembered that between 1940 and 1941 Italians and Germans invaded Greece and raspberry leaf tea was a remedy for diarrhea—things Dunia told him.

He made up a song in honor of his love. Each time Amel whispered, "I love you."

"What else?" she asked.

"I'd die for you," he'd sing.

"What else?"

"You're my whole life."

As a reward, she lessened her resistance. He bought her bags of chips, sugar cookies or chocolate bars every day. She ate his offerings enthusiastically, and then a sudden new craving would pop up. She would get in the mood for yogurt or a chocolate-filled croissant, and he would head back to the store.

He liked her apartment. It was on the second floor of a building built four years earlier and hadn't been lived in for months, empty as a blank page. Watching the dust particles dance like ballerinas in the sunny air, Amel remembered the sand storms of Baghdad. They left so much dust that his mother and sisters swept and mopped from dusk until dawn.

The living room marble floor was like a vanilla and chocolate ice cream swirl, the walls were oak paneling and the balcony door, glass. The kitchen wallpaper was mint with small ivory circles, and its cupboards and floor tiles were dark green. The bedroom was painted white, with a wooden floor and a glass door that led to a second balcony. The bathroom had a bathtub and cockroaches.

Amel met the cockroaches first, but didn't warn Dunia. To him they were as normal as soap bubbles. So when he heard her screaming one night while bathing, he laughed. She came out in a towel, outraged that cockroaches could get as big as hair barrettes. Not until Amel cleared them out did she leave the water puddle under her feet and continue her bath.

Her street was quiet because it was too narrow for cars. Nearby were an orange tree, a bench and the cats that had scared her on her first night. A small café was a little way down, frequented by elderly customers who played with beads.

The kiss not only changed the Athenians, but Amel too. He paid closer attention to the length of her skirts, the depth of her necklines and the shade of her lipstick. If they weren't to his liking, he asked her to change them. He scrutinized any man who came near her, suspicious that those on the trolley leaned against her seat to feel her hair, and those standing at the bus stop intentionally brushed against her back.

In large crowds, especially at the markets, he faced the ordeal of how to have her walk in relation to him. If he positioned her in front, men got an immediate glimpse of her. If she followed behind, they might try to touch her. Walking beside him, they could do both. Unable to make up his mind, he would drag her this way and that, like a doll, and get home feeling as if he had run a marathon.

He never left her alone if he could help it. Once, while he bargained with a vender, she stepped aside to observe the live ducks and chickens on sale. He shouted across the crowd of people for her to return. She obeyed, only to wander off shortly afterwards to a man and pregnant couple selling an antique armchair and lamp. Pushing through buyers and merchants, he went after her, but sensing her agitation he slowed down. He pretended to be piqued by the garbage in the street. "Why don't they clean up here so people can walk?" he asked to save himself.

He wanted to possess her but not anger her. When he did, she either gave him hours of silence or provoked his jealousy more. She would flirtatiously ask a male bus passenger or pedestrian an unnecessary question. Once, while on the metro, she unpinned a blouse she had initially pinned for his sake. When he insisted she pin it back, she dropped the safety pin between the seats.

The kiss had a greater impact on him than it did on her. She never praised him or showed affection. When he asked if she loved him, she ignored the question or plainly said no. As their intimacy progressed to taking off their shirts, she was just as nonchalant. He wondered if even losing her virginity would affect her.

Yet she wore his necklace, a thick gold chain with a cross that his mother gave him before he left Baghdad. Dunia had so admired it that he had taken it off and handed it to her despite her protests.

"Wear it for me," he said. "It'll be safer with you."

Amel wished he could chaperone Dunia in class during the day. Time flew by because he was happy, but he was constantly wondering where she was and what she was doing. Luckily, fear of slicing his hand in one of the machines kept him focused on his work.

Nighttime was good, because he knew she was either visiting Kareema or Najieba. She never went to his place unless he was home. Sabah had been skipping work and she didn't want to be alone with him.

"Sabah said I was in his dream," Dunia told Amel.

Amel was quiet, allowing her to continue.

"He said I was wearing a red nightgown."

"Dunia, I don't want you kidding around with Sabah anymore."

She agreed but asked him not to mention their conversation to Sabah. He said he wouldn't, but the next day he approached Sabah. "Your dreams don't happen to be of red nightgowns lately, do they?"

Turning purple, Sabah dodged the question with a joke. "Hey, have you heard about the Kurd who was walking in the desert? He kept walking and walking and getting more and more tired. So he thought, in order to feel better, he should start running."

Amel didn't laugh and Sabah, turning white, hurried to another machine. Amel was content and reprised the event to Dunia.

"Amel, you told him!"

"So?"

"What did he say?"

"He trembled like a leaf."

From her hidden smile, he knew she was proud that he had stood up for her. He was happy to have had the opportunity.

Dunia never ate dinner until Amel came home from work. After he picked her up from whichever neighbor she was visiting, they bought souvlaki or fried eggs, potatoes or hamburgers. One day Najieba asked Dunia why she didn't cook and save Amel and herself money.

Dunia explained she had never set foot inside her mother's kitchen, but Najieba said that didn't matter. Taking Dunia by the arm, she led her to Amel's kitchen. The only vegetable there was potato. "I'll teach you how to make curry," Najieba said.

When Amel came home that day and saw one pot of curry and one of rice, he was shocked. He knew Sabah wouldn't have cooked and didn't imagine Dunia could have. Excitedly, Dunia ran to him and described what Najieba had said and how she herself had prepared the meal.

"I didn't trust Najieba's measurements—she wanted me to use too much water and too little tomato paste—I made a curry tastier than hers!" Dunia scooped stew from the pot and showed Amel. "See how thick?"

Before he could answer, she grabbed the mismatched dishes from the cupboards and set them on the living room table. Sabah made it home in time to join them. Dunia was happy to be at both men's beck and call.

"You love it, don't you, I know you do," she said, watching them. "Go on, admit it."

"You must first give us a chance to try it, Dunia," Sabah said.

"A chance for what? You've nearly licked your plates clean. I don't need your compliments anyway. I'm well aware of my capabilities. I'm not on the honor roll for nothing."

She kept nagging until they finally admitted how delicious the curry was. Later they all had cocoa at Kareema's. Sabah left before Amel and Dunia, who stayed an hour longer. When they walked out, Amel put his arm around Dunia. As usual, Kareema's daughters peeked and giggled from behind the window. Dunia reminded Amel, more sternly than on other occasions, not to touch her like that in public.

"Like what?" he asked.

"Like a man touches a girl."

"I'm your first cousin."

"So because you're my first cousin, you're safe?"

"Of course."

"So you'd never take advantage of me?"

He stopped and stared hard at her. She turned in the opposite direction and walked fast. "I said nothing wrong," she said. "If you're going to get mad, get mad."

"Come back. The bus stop is on the other side."

"I don't care."

To end her brattiness, he let her go and hastened towards their bus. Dunia called out his name several times, and was then silent. He looked back and saw her sitting on the ground. As he ran to her, she slowly got up and dusted off her pants.

"Are you okay?" he asked.

"My knees are broken," she cried.

He kissed her head. "They're not."

"My ankles are then." She leaned against him and limped. "You're lucky my pants didn't rip. They're one of the few pairs you approve of."

Half the time they were together Amel was too exhausted to go anywhere. Despite her pleas, he avoided making plans. One day, fearing she would end up going on excursions with classmates, he took her to the Acropolis. The problem was he didn't know how to get to the top. Dunia suggested they climb the rocks to catch up with a group of tourists already there, then eavesdrop on their guide. Amel agreed, but not long into the climb he complained the view wasn't worth their efforts.

"It's the Acropolis," she said, "once a place of worship."

"So what?" he asked and tried to tip her over.

She shouted at him, telling him not to play such dangerous games—she could lose her balance and hit her head on the rocks. He pushed her again and she slapped him. Amel told her to wait as he asked a couple to take a picture of them. Dunia posed with him but immediately snapped at him.

They argued until they sprawled on the dirt in fatigue. "I've had enough," he said. "What is all this, anyway? Just a bunch of rocks, rocks, rocks. Everywhere, rocks, rocks."

"Fine, I'll go by myself," she said, walking ahead. He quickly got up and followed but when they reached the top, people were leaving. A sign said the Acropolis closed at 4:00pm.

"How is it closed?" she asked. "There's no fence around it or roof over it. It's right in the open."

She asked Amel if he could tell her anything about the Acropolis. He pursed his lips professorially, straightened imaginary glasses and said, "The Acropolis was built before you and I were born, and people came here to dance around the poles in a circle."

"That's not funny. This was my opportunity to see an important historical site and I missed it."

To make it up to her, he took her to the Herod Atticus Odeum. "In the summer, this is used as a theater."

"What kind of theater?"

"I don't know. Who cares about that? Let's take a picture and go."

On another weekend, they went to the Panathenaic Stadium, where, he explained, the Olympic games were once held. He caught her suppressing a laugh.

"What's so funny?" he asked.

"I came here with a classmate already."

"What classmate?" he asked, fuming.

"Just a classmate."

"Was it a male or female?"

She wouldn't tell him and he couldn't calm down, so that excursion ended quickly.

The weekend after, he took her to the Church of Aghia Paraskevi. They walked a path that wound uphill until they arrived at the chapel, which she compared to the size of his head. "Don't speak like that," he said. "This is an important church."

"Why?" she asked.

"Because!" He gave her two hundred drachmas to deposit so she could make a wish and light a candle.

She pointed to the people at the bottom. "I wish you were down there so I could throw something on your head."

"Stop playing around and pray for something."

"This place isn't worth it. You don't even know what it stands for."

"What a sinner you are."

"Not as big a one as you. Crossing yourself so quickly before you eat it looks as if you're shooing a fly."

Laughing, she ran down the stairs as he chased after her. He couldn't believe how much energy she had. She probably gobbled up eighty percent of all trees' oxygen for herself and gave no carbon dioxide in return. When they got to the bottom, they were breathless. They lay on the grass and Amel took out his pocketknife to scratch their names on one of the rocks.

"Put my name first," she said, but he put his.

On their way home she handed him her purse and said, pointing downhill, "Let's race to the bottom."

"Don't you dare!"

But she was already tearing down the hill. At the bottom, she stopped to catch her breath at a baker's window where she pretended to admire the cakes.

"Come back up!" he called.

"You come down."

He waited in the hope that she would eventually listen, but finally he went down the hill, only to see her running back. They crossed each other half way. Again they were at the opposite ends.

This time, Amel didn't waste time convincing her to follow him. He went after her and she tried to get away but this time he was too quick. Holding her by the arm, he observed her intently and realized from her glowing eyes that even if she made him climb up and down the hill twenty times, he would still end up saying, "I love you, I'd die for you, you're my whole life."

CHAPTER 9

He counted his money, over and over. He could give Dunia a birthday party and buy her a substantial gift if he was willing to take a chance that winter. His paychecks kept him fed properly, but say, God forbid, he lost his job, or his boss cut his hours, then he'd once again have to make broth out of leftover chicken bones.

The weather was changing and winter was quickly approaching but Amel didn't want to think that far ahead. All he wanted was to make Dunia happy. She was against the party. "Let's buy a small cake and eat it alone at my place."

"A party is more fun," he said.

"Not for me."

"Stop interfering," he said.

Amel took her disinclination as modesty. He couldn't believe anyone wouldn't want to celebrate their birthday in splendor. He counted the guests, which included Sabah and Kareema's and Najieba's families, then made a grocery list and ordered a cake from a bakery. On his way to work, he stopped at a couple of jewelers. He settled on a heart shaped gold trinket of the Virgin Mary and chose a gold chain to go with it.

He delegated the purchasing of groceries to Kareema, and the day before the party, he and Dunia went to pick up the cake. When he paid the baker, Dunia looked puzzled. "Amel, that's almost a day's pay. We should've just bought a slice and shared it in private."

"Hush. You're spoiling it for yourself."

The baker gave Dunia a handful of cookies and said something in Greek.

"He says you're pretty," Amel translated for Dunia. "He congratulates you on your birthday and gives you his blessings."

"Thank you," Dunia said to the baker.

After they left, Dunia reprimanded Amel for making such a fuss.

"This is nothing," he boasted. "Wait until you see what else I have for you. Don't beg me to show it to you, though. I won't. Not until tomorrow."

But when they got home he couldn't resist bringing out the jeweler's box.

"But for the life of me, I won't open it." He stared at it proudly. "This cost me a whole week's pay." Then he chuckled, "Who cares, right? It's all gone anyway."

"What are you talking about and why are you laughing?"

"My wallet's empty, but money's no object, right? Your happiness is more important."

"Says who?"

"Says I."

She sighed. "Amel, you never listen to me. That's what I don't like about you."

"What is it that you do like about me?"

She pondered, amusingly. "I love the way you love me."

"What else?"

"I like what your eyes say to me."

"What else?"

"I like that you're an honest, hard-working man."

He glowed like a peacock.

"What I don't like about you is everything else."

The following night, his house—although partly underground—shook from the loud music and children's feet. Najieba's overweight eight-year-old son, Firas, bounced like a giant rabbit from the kitchen to the living room and Amel threatened to send him home without cake if he didn't stop. Firas plopped on the couch, panting and red in the face, and sat still for so long that Dunia suggested he get two slices of cake for good behavior. Then, however, Kareema's daughters and his sisters riled him up again and Amel swore there would be no cake for Firas, as Dunia and Kareema tried to calm him down.

"You don't know what else he did," Amel said. "He dipped his finger in the pilaf."

"No, I didn't!" Firas cried, tucking his head into Dunia's bosom.

"The girls saw you, and there are drops from the pot on your sneakers."

"You can help me blow out the candles, okay?" Dunia intervened, holding up Firas' chin affectionately.

The cake was brought out and the children were warned not to spit on it while blowing out the candles with Dunia. Twirling their fingers and licking their lips, they waited for the song to end. The clapping began, the lights were turned on and the children danced around.

Amel ordered the kids to be quiet as he handed Dunia her gift. He noticed her discomfort opening it in front of everyone, yet he couldn't help feeling proud. When she took the necklace out,

Kareema told Amel to help Dunia put it on. The act resembled that of a couple getting engaged and Sabah cheered the traditional ku-lu-lu-lu-lu as he took pictures. Amel told him to shut up.

After the guests left, Amel and Sabah started to clean up as Dunia watched. She said she was tired and Amel suggested she sleep in his bed. Sabah could take the cot, since she couldn't spend the night in a room with a non-relative. She accepted at once and Sabah couldn't object. It was her birthday.

Even though he was tired too, Amel couldn't fall asleep right away. He thought back on the party and wondered what Dunia really thought of it. From what he observed, it didn't impress her much. Neither did the necklace. She seemed preoccupied throughout. Maybe he shouldn't have pushed her into celebrating her birthday. This was his last thought before he drifted off to sleep.

The next morning Kareema asked to have a word with Amel outside. She hadn't wanted to say anything before the birthday and spoil his mood, but she'd lost some of the money he'd given her to shop with and had to use her own for groceries. She understood it was her fault and didn't expect a drachma from him, but thought he should know, regardless.

Disturbed, Amel simply nodded and went back inside. When Dunia asked what was the matter, he told her the story.

"Are you going to reimburse her?" Dunia asked.

"Why should I? It's not my problem."

"So she had to pay out of her own pocket?" she asked, agitated.

"It was her mistake. Besides, I'm no richer than she is. If her family doesn't have money, it's because her husband is lazy."

Dunia refused to let him touch her that night. She was so angry that whatever he did or said made her snap. He hated days when she was like that, which seemed to come every other week. They flustered him as he waited to see if she would throw him out of her apartment or simply ignore him. When she kicked him out because she had to study or because she wanted her space, it was less scary.

She didn't ask him to get out after her birthday, but the tension between them lasted. She wouldn't say a word to him, while his tongue became as slippery as soap. In an attempt to get her to speak, or at least acknowledge him, he criticized the way she spoke to people. When she snacked, he called her a whale. He said the clothes she tried on made her look fat.

She drew further away from him until he found himself overwhelmed by his own stupidity. He wanted to fix the situation, but getting through her coldness was like tunneling through a mountain.

She spent hours talking nonsense with nobodies but with him she was as silent as pudding. He locked his mouth shut from then on. One night he cleaned her apartment while she bathed. He had done such things before, but usually at her request, not voluntarily. When Dunia stepped out of the bathroom and saw him working, she merely watched, saying nothing. She made tea for them, and they drank it on the bed. She asked if he wanted to hear her speak Greek.

"You don't know Greek," Amel teased, happy she was speaking to him.

"I do now." She recited the phrases she'd picked up.

Amel laughed and kissed her head. "Bravo. You're so smart."

"I am."

"*Sagapou.*"

"What does that mean?"

"You know what it means. I love you."

Blushing, she lowered her eyes.

"Why don't you love me, Dunia?"

"I don't know."

"Did you love your other boyfriends?"

"One boyfriend. And yes, I did. But he was different. We were going to get married."

"What do you think I want to do?"

"You're too young to be my husband."

"Feelings have nothing to do with age. I love you. I always will."

"I didn't come to Greece to find a husband. I came to study."

"I'm not saying now. I want to marry you after I get to America."

"You'll change once you're in America."

"Not me!" he said defensively. "I'll always love you."

"What if you marry someone else?"

"I'll love her like a wife, but not like I love you."

She was quiet.

"I will never love anyone more than I love you," he said. "Before you came, my life was black. One day I took a walk alone and ended up at the Church of Aghia Paraskevi. I thought about climbing to the top and jumping off, but my love for my family stopped me. Since you came, I've forgotten my mother, my father. I know only you now."

"You don't know me as a person."

"I know enough. You're not like other Chaldean girls in America."

"How do you know? You haven't met them."

"I've seen plenty—those who came to Baghdad before the war, and the ones who visit Athens. They are conceited, superficial, and they expect everyone to cater to them."

"Chaldean men from America have those traits too. You might adopt them one day."

"Impossible!"

"Is that why you love me—because I'm different in that way?"

"No," he answered.

She caressed her left leg in meditation. Her skin smelled of coconut and aloe, and her wet hair of lemon.

"I know what I want career-wise," she said as if to herself. "Everything else is on hold. Romance doesn't necessarily mean love, let alone marriage."

Her coldness surprised him. If he was hit by a taxi tomorrow, she would attend class as usual then come to the hospital after visiting hours were over. "Am I anything to you?" he asked.

She laughed. "Of course. You see past what I say and you don't focus on my looks. It's true that you don't understand my ambitions but you make up for it by marinating my heart with affection."

He was so touched he grabbed her hand. "Will you ever marry me, Dunia?"

"You're talking how many years from now?" she asked, raising her brows. "We live in different countries. You don't even have a phone."

He was saddened by the heavy complications. For a while they sipped their tea in silence.

"Why didn't you marry the man you loved?" he asked.

Her eyes momentarily twitched at the question, then returned to normal. "I think his family thought I was too sexy to be a wife."

"He's a loser."

She meditated a while. "Amel, why do you love me?"

"I just do."

"But why?"

"I don't know."

"Then what is it that you love most about me?"

"I love all of you," he said.

"There must be a part of me you prefer."

"What are you, a chicken and I have to choose between the wing or leg?" he asked.

Placing her cup on the floor, Dunia gently took his tea as well. She leaned towards him. "Maybe in the future—maybe when I finish school—maybe if your circumstances change...."

She stopped talking and kissed him passionately.

CHAPTER 10

A month before the holidays, Amel's schedule changed. He worked fifteen- to seventeen-hour shifts and had no days off. Sundays were half days, but they didn't relieve his aches and pains. He was so tired when he got home that all he could do was eat his meal and close his eyes. When Dunia was around, he was able to rejuvenate his senses through hers.

Although it was a mess, her apartment was his haven. Books were spread out on the furniture and floor, fruit, bread, cheese and butter always left out on the kitchen counter. Her numerous toiletries, rarely used, cluttered the bathroom.

He would ask, if he wasn't too exhausted to speak, about her day. Now that Sabah had gotten a new job, and hadn't started skipping work yet, she usually spent her time outside of school and the cafés at his house. Kareema and Najieba gave her recipes, and their children, who were first to know she was in and knock on her door, greatly entertained her.

Najieba's two-year-old, Fatin, and Kareema's youngest, Maram, were Dunia's favorites. Fatin's hair was so tightly curled and overgrown that it looked like a bush. Maram, soft and shy, spoke mostly with her bright blue eyes. Because Maram was Amel's favorite too, he and Dunia often teased her by trying to make her pick which of them she liked best.

Najieba's son, Firas, had his own collection of stunts. Arms spread out, he stood on his chubby toes and danced ballet. Dunia was so tickled she took pictures of him performing to take back to America for when she would need a good laugh. Kareema's middle daughter liked brushing Dunia's hair and chopping onions, while the oldest girls in each family were simply nuisances. They would dig through her school bag and purse and ask if they could have her scrunchie, eraser or pencil sharpener.

Amel knew the approximate time she would be in the neighborhood, and was able to contact her occasionally. He'd call the kiosk down the block, leave a message with the clerk, who in turn gave it to one of Kareema's or Najieba's children—his frequent customers—and then they'd run with it to Dunia. This gave him peace of mind. Amel was surprised when one day over dinner, Dunia said she was going with her class to the Greek islands.

"I want to see them before I go back home," she said.

Prior to her announcement his thoughts never extended beyond basic survival.

"Which class is going?" he asked.

She laughed. "It's not for only one class, Amel. It's for whomever is in the study-abroad program."

"When are they going?"

"Next week."

"You just found out about it today?"

"I've known about it, but I hadn't thought about it much. I've been busy with homework and tests."

"Did you already book?"

"I signed my name."

"When?"

"Today."

Amel was upset and didn't hide it. He stopped eating and stared at his plate. She kindly asked if he was full, and whether he wanted fruit, which made him more suspicious. He said no and went to wash up in the bathroom. Looking in the mirror, he saw his veins enlarging.

Since she had started attending the university, he hadn't once checked out her classes, fellow students or teachers. He was uncertain about what was going on. Why had she kept the trip a secret, if that was what she had done? He had no evidence to accuse her of betraying him, but why did he have this fear crawling up his spine?

The next few minutes felt like an eternity. He had to decide whether to interrogate her then and there and chance her anger, or wait. The former might confirm his worst suspicions and the latter could age him quickly.

Both options terrified him. His instinct prevailed—he quizzed her that night. From what he gathered, the trip was five days long, cost two hundred dollars, was supervised by university professors, and of course, the hotel rooms were gender segregated.

Everything she said made the trip sound safe and ideal, but he still wasn't at ease. The next day he left a message from work. When Dunia called back he asked her if she had told her parents about her trip to the islands.

"Not yet," she said. "I planned on calling them once I'm done with this big paper that's due."

"I think you should get their permission before you book."

"I doubt they'll say no. No one comes all the way to Greece and skips the islands."

He paused. "Are you allowed to bring friends?"

"What do you mean?"

"I mean, can I come?"

"What about work?"

"I've been working so hard my back will break. I need a vacation."

"Amel, your boss won't let you leave an hour before your shift ends and you want five whole days off?"

She was right, but he could quit. Lots of places were hiring cheap labor. He could work with Sabah, building picture frames. There were fewer hours but that was good. He was tired of the drudgery and a boss who talked of trees as though they were his family.

"I thought you once told me it isn't safe for you to travel. You could be caught by immigration."

"I asked my boss and he says they don't send refugees back unless they do something illegal."

He felt her taking a deep breath, and knew what was coming. "I think we should talk about this later," he said.

"What's wrong?"

"Nothing, but I'm holding up the phone."

"I'll try to get off work early...."

"No, don't do that. Stay until the regular time."

At home, neither said a word. He wanted her to speak first so he'd have the upper hand.

"So," she said, pinching the hamburger with her fork, "you want to risk your job for a five-day vacation."

"If I don't go while you're here, I'll never go at all."

"You'd feel comfortable with my classmates?"

"You spend twice as much time with them as you do with me."

"If you get fired on account of your jealousy, I will stop talking to you completely."

The subject was closed. He didn't pursue the issue and went to bed with a headache. Maybe she was doing him some good, he considered. The last thing he needed was to lose his job. His money was almost gone. Aside from what he spent on her birthday, he bought Dunia lots of souvlakis and treats, and whenever she forgot to go to a bank and exchange her dollars; he left her a sum of drachmas on her nightstand.

Amel was confused; he couldn't decide whether to be happy or sad about being coerced not to go on the trip.

They spent Sunday at his house so she could say goodbye to the neighbors before she left for the islands Monday morning. Hakeem brought over cocoa and they all drank and made jokes about Athenians and Kurds. Dunia was asked which islands she was going to, what time her ferry left, where her class was meeting. Amel listened to each answer carefully. They were first going to Mykonos, and from there, to Santorini.

"Who's driving you to Piraeus?" Hakeem asked.

"They've rented a bus," Dunia said.

"Poor Amel," Kareema said. "What will he do without you? Who will cook for him?"

Najieba and Sabah volunteered, but Amel said he could do it himself.

"Ah, then poor Sabah," Dunia teased.

Amel didn't think that was funny and he let her know it with his glare.

"I bet you miss your mother's potato chops and *irook*, Amel, don't you?" Najieba asked.

"Don't mention those dishes," Sabah said. "What's worse is not tasting *kubba, pacha, harrisa*." Shaking his head, he rubbed his stomach. "I lived like a king in Baghdad, I swear."

"You wish," Amel said. "You act like your mother cooked those meals every day. She might've made them once a year, if you were lucky."

"You think so, huh? My mom made *pacha* once a month."

Amel laughed. "I'm sure you haven't had *pacha* for so long, you've forgotten it's made of stuffed sheep stomach skin or rubber."

"What, you think we couldn't afford *pacha?* At least when we made it, we invited relatives. Your family hoarded it like gold."

"We're your relatives. We were never invited."

The women tried to break up their squabble by changing the subject. Dunia remained uninvolved. Amel wished she would put a word in, so he could say what he wanted to her. On the way to her place, she didn't ask a single question. It was as though nothing strange had happened between him and Sabah. Under normal circumstances, she would ask what was bothering him and why had he picked on Sabah.

"Why aren't you packing?" he asked, before they got into bed.

"I have time tomorrow."

"Why wouldn't you pack tonight?"

"It's two o'clock and I can't keep my eyes open. I'm only taking a couple of things. I can throw them in my school bag in a few minutes."

She turned off the lights and got under the covers, her back turned towards him. Amel tossed and turned, hoping to catch her attention. But she ignored him. "Dunia," he finally called.

"Yes?"

"Don't go."

She was quiet a while, then asked, "Where?"

"To the islands."

"You can't be serious. My ticket will go to waste."

"So what?"

"It's worth two hundred dollars. More than that."

"So what?"

She stared at the ceiling in wonder. "Why don't you want me to go?"

"I don't know."

She didn't complain that he was being irrational, and she didn't get mad. He knew something wasn't right, but he had no proof. She was smart, but he wasn't stupid. Just because she could pronounce the name of the Greek president better and knew that eggplants were members of the night-shade family and relatives of potatoes didn't mean she could dupe him. She might have book knowledge, but he had undergone travails beyond her understanding.

She was sleeping when he left before sunrise. They hadn't said goodbye properly, but he didn't dare wake her up. Ever since he turned her trip into an interrogation, he sensed her avoiding him.

At work, Amel didn't feel well. Large vines twisted in his stomach and a sack of potatoes sat in his head. He didn't know how he would manage the days without her. He was consumed by what she might be doing.

CHAPTER 11

She returned sweetened, her complexion as clear and vibrant as a fresh apple. There was a harmony between her and the breeze. But toward him, she was as sour as a lemon. She flinched at the sound of his approach, fueling his turmoil. No longer could he discount what might have occurred.

He made several attempts to get her to tell him the truth, but she maneuvered herself into different activities to avoid him. She played Tetris, hid in the kitchen, took naps, studied. Occasionally he considered disregarding her evasions. She was returning to America in twenty-two days and was busy studying, shopping for gifts and clothes and seeing as much of Greece as she could.

But knowing the truth was essential to his health. It related to his faith and religion, to his sanity. But her shell was hard, and she must have sensed his intentions because with each attempt he made, she beat him to the punch by hurling insults.

He decided to change tactics. He would come home unexpectedly and call into work sick. He even entered a telephone booth with her while she spoke to her family.

"Can I have some privacy?" she asked, stomping her feet. He kicked the booth's corner, then went outside and sat on a curb. Watching her dial the numbers, he pricked up his ears. The only sounds he heard were car and motorcycle engines. Soon she came out.

"No one was home," she said. "I'll call later today."

He could tell by her nonchalance she was lying. And although he didn't hear her speak, he'd seen her lips move. He wanted to accuse her right there and then, but she turned to him and smiled sadly. "I'm leaving in less than three weeks, can you believe it?"

He was in awe. How she turned from a poisonous plant into a flower was beyond him. Whether she was sincere or not didn't make a difference. The fact was her departure was close. He remembered the days before she arrived, when life was frustrating and pointless. Now he was sad. He regretted having obsessed on her five-day trip, negating the months of exhilaration she had given him.

Perhaps he was wrong.

"I'm going to try my family again," she shouted later in the day, while he was in the washroom doing laundry. He dropped the clothes in the tub and ran out. She was already gone.

He rushed to the nearest telephone booth. She wasn't there. He raced towards one farther down the street, and slowed when he saw her back. He stepped lightly towards the booth, until his face was pressed against the window. She was absorbed in her conversation and was unaware of his presence at first. She shifted and saw him.

His presence shocked her, strangling her giggles and smile, but she retrieved her boldness quickly enough. Acting calm, she turned her back to him. He banged on the glass until she hung up and stormed out of the booth.

"How dare you sneak up on me like that?" she shouted, marching ahead without looking at him. "That was low and childish. You suffocate me." She abruptly stopped and faced him. "What is it you want? Why do you act like we're a couple when we're not? I'm leaving soon, you know. You have no rights over me."

He was in such rage, he wanted to burn down Athens.

"I need time alone, understand?"

He huffed and puffed.

"Unless you behave in a civilized manner, I don't want you to come over anymore," she said. "You're affecting my concentration and ruining my last days in Athens."

Amel ran a fever for two days. In a way it was good—his high temperature killed his desire to crush the truth out of her.

His boss was throwing a Christmas party at work. He spent a week's pay on a jacket from Monastiraki and pants from a tailor down the street. He was looking forward to telling Dunia about the party, because she never went anywhere fun at night. She had begged him several times to take her to clubs but he refused. Giving her permission, let alone leading her into such places, was too disgraceful to even consider. If her mother in America heard, she would say he had failed to keep her safe and protect her reputation.

She wore a red velvet dress with Chinese patterns; it was short, had long sleeves and a square neckline. Amel was startled—he'd forgotten how beautiful she was. As her personality had unrolled like a carpet over the months, he had taken her looks for granted.

They took the bus to the shop and Amel proudly showed her the recent display sets he had worked on: bed posts, dresser, kitchen table and a desk. He described how each was built and the time it required to make it. Amel felt like an artist in love with his canvas.

Amel wondered what would have happened to him if he hadn't concentrated on getting to America. Would he be at a university in Baghdad? What if he had been born in America? Would he have become a doctor or lawyer? If Dunia, a female, could enter any field, think what he could have done. The possibilities were mind-boggling. But now he had to concentrate on the present. The hors d'oeuvres were disappearing quickly, and he planned on having quite a few in order to save on dinner.

Dunia met his boss and his boss's wife at the buffet. The boss was so friendly, patting him on the back and praising him, that Amel got annoyed—he was impatient to stack food on the plates. Finally, his boss mingled with other employees and Amel got to efficiently arrange the *spanakopitta, keftedes,* braised artichokes, lunchmeat, dips and bread so nothing would tip over.

Then he led Dunia into a corner, separated from everyone else. From a safe distance, he acquainted her with his co-workers. "The three men behind us," he said, eating a *spanakopitta,* "the ones with their wives and children, they're Egyptians, but Christian. They're excellent people."

"I thought all Egyptians were Muslim."

"No, not all."

"Why don't we go and talk to them?"

He raised his eyebrows in disapproval. "It's better that we don't." Suddenly he realized he hadn't brought soda. He took her half-empty plate. "I'll be right back."

"None for me, Amel," she said.

"Why not? I was going to get you a soda too."

"I don't like soda. But I'll have some more of that spinach pie. And do they have champagne?"

He paused. "You're serious?"

"Never mind," she said.

When he returned, he handed her her plate and a glass of soda.

"I told you I didn't want one," she said.

"I got you one, anyway. Is that okay with you?"

"No, it's not."

"If it was champagne, it would be okay?"

Rolling her eyes, she turned her head the other way. He swore at himself for upsetting her. He had striven so hard, suppressed his anger for the sake of making her happy, and yet one wrong word and she couldn't forgive him.

When they got home, he tiptoed around her bad mood. She changed into her nightgown, brushed her teeth and got into bed. Then she told Amel she didn't want him to spend the night.

This took him off guard. Normally the latest she kicked him out was at 11:50pm; when there was just time to catch a bus. It was 12:10am, and busses weren't running.

"Dunia, it's very hard to get a taxi this time of night," he said.

"This is the weekend. Buses run until one o'clock."

Her intelligence never ceased to amaze him, and neither did his stupidity. He sat beside her on the bed. "What's the matter, Dunia?"

"I want to be alone."

He rested his head on her shoulder.

"Amel, what did I just say?" she asked, tensely.

Sighing in frustration, his eyes turning red, he didn't move, hoping she would soften. She did the opposite. She used harsher words to express how badly she wanted him to leave. When he still didn't budge, she got up and started to dress.

"I'm going for a walk," she said.

He shifted a bit. "I'll come with you."

"No! I want to be alone."

"It's almost midnight. It's not safe."

"Then leave!"

Now he had to stay with her for a different reason—she was so hysterical he was afraid to leave her alone.

"Let me come with you," he begged.

Turning her face to the ceiling, she moaned in despair. "Please Amel, I need my space. Let me get some fresh air, on my own."

"Not this late, Dunia."

All of the sudden she exploded like a firecracker. "You are so narrow-minded, you don't see how different we are. You assume what makes you happy makes me happy. I didn't want the birthday party!"

He felt cooked. She had flipped and pressed him like a hamburger.

"My God, Amel, you've blown what we have together out of proportion. Everyone thinks we're engaged. You've used our family connection to your advantage and overlooked what's good for me!"

Each and every word aged him. Now he too needed space and fresh air.

She changed into her nightgown again and got into bed. "Happy? I'm not going out, but you're not staying—even if this drags on until three in the morning."

"Why are you doing this to me, Dunia?"

"What am I doing to you? I want to be alone. What's that got to do with you?"

He brooded over what to do. Leaving her in this condition was irresponsible, but inevitable. Her insults were accumulating, like ants over a crumb. Each second seemed like an hour and so, eventually, his legs directed him out the door.

He cried on the way home. Why had she been so cruel? Yes, he drove her mad but she could have been gentler, too. She had drained his spirit. When he reached home, he collapsed into bed and fell into a deep, dreamless sleep.

He arrived at her apartment at 6:30pm the next day, but she wasn't home. He stopped at his house then followed the sound of girls' laughter to Kareema's. Dunia was there. Hakeem was preparing to make cocoa and everyone else was huddled on the couch.

"You're off late for a Sunday," Kareema said as she hemmed a pleated skirt.

"I came from her place," he said, motioning to Dunia. "I didn't know she'd be here."

"You missed Dunia last night. She came knocking at your door long after midnight." Kareema cut the black thread with her teeth. "You didn't hear, though. You must have been dreaming of pickled mangos."

Kareema's daughters giggled, and Amel looked at Dunia in disbelief. She blushed and lowered her eyes.

"We pleaded with her to spend the night at our house, but she refused." Kareema held the skirt up and observed it. "She said she was just in the area and thought to stop by."

"So how was the party last night?" Hakeem asked, setting up his burner in the middle of the living room.

Amel smiled at Dunia, and avoided the question. "Today my boss came up to me," he said instead. "He wanted to know who the girl with me was. I told him my cousin, the one from America. He couldn't believe it."

"Yes, she could pass for Greek or Italian, couldn't she?" Hakeem said.

"It's not that," Amel said. "He was stunned that someone as beautiful as her, and from America could be related to someone like me, who doesn't have two cents in his pockets and is as pretty as a rat."

Everyone but Dunia, who continued to blush, laughed. Hakeem brought out peanuts and insisted that Amel and Dunia stay for cocoa. So Amel could fit, Manal sat on the arm of the couch, Maysoon climbed on the back, and Maram snuggled beside Dunia. Amel asked Maram if she had dumped him for Dunia, and when she said yes, he called her a traitor. He also pinched Manal's arm because she was whining too much and hurting his ears. Meanwhile, Hakeem stirred the cocoa and ridiculed Kareema's uncle in America.

At ten o'clock, Amel and Dunia left.

"Why did you leave me yesterday?" she asked.

"Dunia, you told me to."

"So what? You still shouldn't have left."

"It was what you wanted."

"It was not. I thought you knew me enough by now to know that." His arms around her shoulders, he hugged her and kissed her head.

"You were cruel," she went on. "Leaving me as you did on a Saturday night, all alone. Why didn't you come back? I was expecting you."

He kissed her head again.

"I cried after you left, you know. I felt bad and hoped you'd come back so I could apologize. You didn't, so I came to you."

"You should've stayed at Kareema's."

"How could I when five of them share one bed and a couch? It wasn't that bad, anyway, except for the ride home. I was on the bus with only one other guy. He kept leering at me and smirking. I couldn't tell if he was trying to scare me for fun or for real."

He sighed, and they exchanged looks that said how sorry each was. At home they ate tangerines and went to bed early. Dunia cuddled beside him. Soon she was crying, her tears bathing his face.

Amel begged to know what was wrong, but she wouldn't say. At each plea, her tears multiplied. "Please Dunia, tell me. I'll do anything to make you happy."

"I don't want anything," she said, swallowing to clear her voice. "But tell me, Amel, do you still love me?"

"I never stopped."

"But do you love me?"

"I would die for you. You are my life."

"No, no, tell me if you love me."

"Of course, I do. Of course, I love you."

"And no matter what I do, you'd still love me?"

"You know I will," he said, wiping her tears and kissing her cheeks. "Now please, don't cry. I can't bear to see you cry."

"And no matter what I'd done, you'd still love me?"

"Dunia, stop crying. You're killing me."

"No matter what? Tell me, no matter what?"

"No matter what."

"Are you sure?"

"Oh, Dunia, Dunia, Dunia," he said, pressing her against his chest.

He watched her fall asleep. Suddenly her education, her intelligence, her being American no longer intimidated him. The stickiness of her dried tears, the dampness of her hair and lashes, her tranquility as she slept, made Amel realize she had not lost her innocence. Here she was, with her college prospects and U.S. citizenship, thirsting for love and comfort like a baby.

CHAPTER 12

The room was as dark as a cave. Light came from the bathroom door, where he had groomed himself. He dressed while she lay in bed, sheets twisted around her left leg like grapevines. He sat at the edge of the bed and watched her. Soon she would be gone. He would be an empty cabinet again.

Dunia woke and smiled drowsily.

"I don't want to leave you alone," he said.

"You do that every day," she laughed lightly. "What's the difference now?"

He was quiet, weighing the dangers.

"Besides, I have a long day today," she said. "I'll be in the library until late."

"Don't go anywhere afterwards. I'll meet you here."

When he returned at ten o'clock, the place was empty. His heart beat as he imagined her jumping off the Acropolis or in front of a trolley. He should search the university. Perhaps she had found solitude in an empty classroom or she might be buying roasted chestnuts from her favorite cart near Omonia Square, at the entrance of the metro.

He fried four eggs and two hamburger patties to maintain his composure. It would take him a week to search all those places. At least if he cooked, dinner would be ready for her when she returned. She walked in at 10:30.

She was breathless, her hair frizzy, her skin dark from dust and fumes. "You won't believe why I'm late...."

He walked up to her and patted her hair. "Where have you been? I was worried about you."

"Nowhere special. If it hadn't been for the traffic, I would've been here way ahead of you."

"That's okay. I'm not mad."

She pondered. "Why aren't you mad?"

"Because I was worried instead. I've been sitting here thinking the worst."

"Like what?"

"I don't know. I thought maybe you did something stupid. You should've heard yourself last night."

Her hand on her chest, she laughed. "You thought I'd killed myself?"

He ignored her and went to bring the food from the kitchen. She followed him, wrapping her arms around his stomach and kissing his cheeks. "You thought I was dead, didn't you? And you felt bad because you assumed you drove me to it?"

"Hand me the salt," he said, smiling.

When they sat down to eat, he saw a designer bag beside her school bag. "What's in that bag?" he asked.

"Oh, just a Christmas ornament a clerk gave me from his shop."

"And why would a clerk do that for you?"

"Because he saw how pretty I am and wanted to go to bed with me."

The bread he had dipped in the egg yolk hung in the air as he stopped to frown at her.

She rolled her eyes. "He knew I was from America and gave it to me as a souvenir. Anything wrong with that?"

"How did he know you were from America?"

"I told him."

"How did you two start talking to begin with?"

"He spoke to me in Greek, as Greeks often do, and I told him I wasn't Greek."

"And then you felt the need to tell your whole life story?"

"No, but he was friendly so we carried on a friendly conversation."

"So every man who has talked to you in Greek, you've made friends with?"

"No. Only the young and handsome ones."

Amel reached over the table and pulled a strand of her hair. She looked over her shoulder. "Did you get egg on me?" she asked.

"I used my clean hand."

She sniffed her hair. "It smells greasy."

He didn't argue, but knew how to get revenge. In the morning, while tying his shoes, an accident occurred. He didn't tell Dunia about it, but when he came home she was waiting for him. "You crushed my Christmas ornament!"

He opened a cupboard. "Don't we have tomatoes? When was the last time you went grocery shopping? I left a bunch of drachmas for you yesterday."

"My beautiful ornament," she cried. "Look at it."

He looked at the shattered blue glass.

"You did it on purpose, didn't you?"

He shouldn't have smiled, he thought, even as he denied doing it and hurried out of her sight.

Dunia's classes ended, and Amel was relieved. Her schoolwork amounted to a full-time job. During exams she was so irritable he couldn't come within ten feet of her. Between exams she roamed the streets of Athens or sat in cafes, swinging her legs and chewing on her pencil. He would have loved to have been a part of that, but he was never invited. Sometimes he thought of catching her off guard by showing up at a class. Would she be welcoming, flustered or angry?

Had his boss been more flexible and Dunia less of a temper, Amel would have done it. His curiosity about what she had done in her five days in the islands hadn't died yet. If it weren't for her outburst after the Christmas party, he would have dug deeper into the truth. Nonetheless, he was glad the semester was over and she had no excuse to come home late.

The closer it came to her departure, the more Amel watched the clock. At his request, Dunia had changed her ticket from December 22nd to the 27th, so she could spend Christmas with him and New Year's Eve with her family. The delivery orders at work were still high but production slowed down. Saturday shifts were cut in half, and he wasn't scheduled every Sunday. Whenever his boss was in a good mood, Amel asked to leave early. The presence of Christmas trees must have a powerful impact on him, Amel thought.

Her last week in Athens, he asked her to be home by six, since he didn't know which day his boss would be nice enough to let him off. She promised she would. "I don't believe you," he said.

"Amel, I swear! I'll be here by six."

"Everyday?"

"I can't guarantee everyday, but today for sure."

At seven o'clock, no one was home. She broke her oath, he murmured, kicking the wall and damaging his weak shoe. He hunted frantically for a pen and paper, and wrote, "Thank you for waiting."

He placed the note on the table, and left. He wasn't stepping foot inside her apartment again. If she wanted to see him, she could come to him—he was sick and tired of chasing after her. She had a heart of ebony. Maybe his boss could use it, carve it into a bowl or something. Her and her ridiculous education! No one cared about the emperors of Ethiopia, German physicists, the families of cabbages or what happened in 1945.

At home he couldn't unlock his door. He had left his key beside the note. Sabah wasn't home, and it was getting cold as Firas walked up and asked why he was standing around like a monkey. Amel examined Firas' white teeth, glistening in the dark. He was crunching a freshly pealed carrot and Amel remembered his last meal was nine hours ago. His stomach growled.

"Give me that carrot," he said.

Firas batted an eye. "Yeah, right."

"Give me the carrot, you need to diet anyway."

"Carrots are for skinny people."

"Exactly, so give me that." Amel snatched the carrot and as he walked away, Firas threatened that if he didn't repay him with a bag of chips, he would tell on him.

Amel calmed down during the ride back to Dunia's, and started twirling his toes. She would punish him severely for having stood up for himself. He would be lucky if she let him in her apartment.

He tried buzzing himself in, but she didn't answer. Her lights were off, so he figured she must be sleeping. He stood beneath her bedroom balcony and threw pebbles at the glass door while calling out her name. After a long while, he heard, "What do you want?"

"You have something of mine."

"Tell me what it is and I'll throw it to you."

"I want to get it myself."

"I throw it to you, or you don't get it at all."

"Dunia, please."

"No."

"Open the damn door."

"I won't."

"You will."

"We'll see," she said.

He kicked the wall. "I left my house key on your table."

Her bedroom light came on. The balcony door cracked open slightly and a broom swept his key outside. The lights turned off as he picked up the key. "Dunia, let me in, I want to talk to you." She didn't answer. "Come on, I look like a fool in front of the neighbors."

"Good!"

"Please, I'm freezing."

Finally, she buzzed him in. He ran through the dark hallway and up the staircase to her front door, which was ajar. She was in her room, hiding under a tent of bed covers.

"Why didn't you let me in?" he asked, sitting down.

"Because I hate you."

He sighed heavily.

"A lot," she added.

"Come out from underneath the covers."

"No, you know what you did and I'm never talking to you again."

"You made me wait over an hour."

"That's not what I'm talking about."

"Then what is it?"

She stuck her head out and sat up straight. "You know what it is."

"I don't know."

"What about the key?"

"What about it?"

"Why did you leave it beside the note?"

"I didn't leave it, I forgot it."

"You expect me to believe that?"

"Why else would I leave my house key?" he asked.

"Your house key?"

He was confused. "You thought it was my key to your apartment? Why would I do that?"

"If it's the key to your house, why did it take you so long to come back for it?"

"I waited for Sabah a while, then I grabbed a bite to eat."

"Liar!"

"I don't lie. What, you thought I left my key to your apartment to say I wasn't coming back anymore?"

She lowered her eyes. "That wasn't your message?"

"Of course not."

Suddenly, she grinned. "I should've figured. You're not that smart."

Smiling, he embraced her. With her frizzy thick hair and smooth skin she felt like a puppy in his arms. "Dunia, I won't be able to buy you a Christmas gift," he said apologetically.

"Don't be silly. You've done enough already."

"I hate life here. In Iraq, even during the war, we didn't celebrate Christmas without new clothes and gifts." They were quiet a while before he added, "I don't know if I'll ever see my family again."

"Amel, don't say that."

"God knows when I'll get to America, and once I do, it'll be years before they follow. If I'm stuck here, it'll be a miracle if we see each other at all."

"Can't they come here?"

"I won't let my family live in such poverty," he said. "Imagine, leave Baghdad to sleep under damp roofs, on paper-thin mattresses, to look in shop windows and drool over what they can't have."

They lay quiet for some time.

"Dunia, can you stay?" he asked.

"What do you mean?"

"For another semester? Can you stay?"

"I've thought of it, but it's expensive. My parents helped me out this time, but I don't think they'll agree to another semester unless I pay for it myself."

"You don't have to study, you can just stay. I'll give you expense money."

"I can't accept your help. You can't afford it." She pondered. "On the other hand, with my education and language skills, I could get a good job and take care of both our rents."

"Doing what?"

"I'll be a nanny."

"Don't be crazy."

"I'm not crazy."

"You are if you want to work as a maid."

"A nanny is not a maid."

"Dunia, stop it."

"Okay, then find me a job."

He laughed. "Oh sure, maybe at the furniture shop so the guys can watch you instead of the machines."

"Amel, I answered an ad I saw on the campus bulletin board," she confessed. "They want an English-speaking nanny for a five-year-old girl. The husband works in the day but his wife is always home, so I won't baby-sit the child, just teach her English and watch her when the mother wants to be alone. It's a great opportunity, only it's a little far from Athens—in Kifissia."

"Kifissia?"

"Yes, you know it?"

"It's two hours from here."

"The man said an hour and a half."

"Two," he emphasized. "And even if it's an hour and a half, you'll be spending the whole time commuting."

"I can move there."

He looked at her in disbelief.

"He's willing to pay me thirty thousand drachmas a week!"

"No, absolutely not."

"There's no shame in working, Amel."

"Working where you live, near your family, is one thing. Working in a foreign country is another."

"It amounts to the same thing. Making money."

"You came here to study, not work."

"If I plan to stay, I'll have to work."

"Then go back."

"What?"

"Go back. I won't encourage you to do what's wrong for my sake."

"You're a liar," she stormed. "You're afraid I might upset your peace of mind if you can't watch my every move. All you think about is yourself."

"That's not true, and you know it."

"It is true. You'd rather get rid of me than put up with me."

"You know I'd give my life for you, but you must go back. Your education is your priority. Losing a semester will hurt. You belong with your family, focusing on your future, Dunia, not living like me. I'm so unsettled I don't have a single certainty about tomorrow."

She slid off the bed and came to his side. Kneeling in front of him, she kissed his face as old women did pictures of saints. Then she burst into tears and hugged him with all her might.

CHAPTER 13

mel assembled a liquor cabinet. He was sad. Sawdust from the shop rained on his clothes like his renewed worries. Soon Dunia would be gone and so would his joy in being in Athens. He decided if his relatives didn't get him out of Greece soon, he would return to Iraq.

"Demitri," he heard his boss shout over the loud noises. "Demitri, *tilefono.*"

It was his mother. She wanted to wish him a merry Christmas ahead of time, since he was off during the holidays. She hadn't spoken to his aunts and uncles in a while, but hoped to do so before Christmas or the New Year. She asked about her niece, and Amel confessed his affection for her, praised her qualities. He said Dunia was the best girl he had ever laid eyes on. He could not believe a Chaldean from America could be so clever, yet humble and amiable.

"*Youm,* I love her," he said.

"Are her feelings mutual?" she asked.

"Not yet. I asked if she'd marry me and she said she might after she graduates from law school."

"A decent man would allow her to finish her education."

"She says she didn't come to Greece to find a husband, but to study."

"No one can predict God's will."

"I'm thinking she'll be better able to sort things out when she's with her family, away from me."

"My sister would be overjoyed by the idea. Your father's siblings would too."

"It's not that. You'll understand later."

"Don't be so doubtful. She may be written for you. It's no coincidence that God brought her to Athens."

The static died.

"Hello? Hello?"

He hung up the phone and returned to work feeling stronger. His circumstances had restrained him from taking his own proposal seriously. He had forgotten he had wealthy aunts and uncles eager to support him financially. His mother had given him hope for the possibility that Dunia would marry him.

Maybe it was God's will that they be husband and wife. God created beads of different size and color and chose which went on what string to form what necklace. Amel suddenly believed he and Dunia would end up on the same thread. True, she said she didn't love him, but given all her contradictions and uncertainties, maybe she did. Foreign lands did strange things to people.

They spent Christmas Day at Amel's house. He invited the neighbors for lunch and they all brought food. During tea, Dunia passed out gifts to everyone but Sabah. It was improper for a girl to give a single man, especially a non-relative, a gift. Feeling left out, Sabah said he was meeting up with friends and left early. When Kareema's and Najieba's families left, Amel thanked Dunia but told her she needn't have.

"I liked shopping for you," she said.

He looked at the two sweaters and the watch she had bought him. He had seen them in her closet and she had claimed they were for her brothers. "You were able to fool me."

"I know," she said.

They were invited to his cousin Shams' house for dinner. Shams and Amel had made up at church, after Midnight Mass. Dunia and Amel wanted to rest first, so they lay on the couch in the dark as the furnace blew heat against them.

"I'm going to miss you," Amel said, half asleep. "You gave me the best days of my life."

"How do you know? You still have thousands left."

"I just know."

"How?"

"I know."

They spent the next day in Plaka and Kolonaki Square. She bought souvenirs and a black dress for a New Year Eve's party her family would attend. At twenty thousand drachmas, the dress was a great bargain and so beautiful on her it made Amel's eyes blurry.

"You looked like a cake," he said, when they walked out of the boutique. "But my love, wasn't the slit too high?"

She laughed. "Not in America."

"Don't dream you'll dress like that after we marry."

"I will dress like that always, even during court trials. And who said we're going to get married? That subject must remain closed until I graduate from law school."

He smiled. "I kind of mentioned us to my mother."

"Amel, you didn't!"

"She was happy as could be."

"But you know I hate people knowing about us."

"Why? I'm in love with you and I want to share that with the people dearest to me."

Seeing her distraught expression, he asked, "You think this was news to her?"

"How else would she have known?"

"When your mother visited Baghdad and I saw your picture, I asked for your hand in marriage. I was told to wait until I got to America."

She seemed light headed, and Amel didn't know if it was due to what he had said or fatigue.

"Why didn't my mother tell me?"

"Our moms didn't take me seriously, probably laughed behind my back."

"Why didn't you tell me?"

He kicked a rock. "I felt silly."

"Oh, Amel," she said, her hand over her forehead. "Your love is going to wreck my plans."

He was bloated with bliss. To be safe he kept quiet.

"Do you still carry that picture?"

"I lost it on the way to Athens."

"You really shouldn't have told your mother," she said. "Now she's going to tell your relatives."

"No, she won't."

Dunia didn't look at all convinced, but that only amplified his joy. If his mother told his aunts and uncles, and they, through their influence, became actively involved, his love affair with Dunia was sure to continue.

When Kareema and Hakeem heard about the dress Dunia bought they asked her to model it for them. She did, and Kareema's first question was, "Isn't it a bit tight—around the stomach?"

"I could wear a corset, I suppose."

"Congratulations," Hakeem said, and Kareema echoed him.

"The dress isn't tight," Dunia said to Amel when they left Kareema's house. "That's the style. It's not for rock climbing, it's for a party."

"So she doesn't know. What do you care?"

She scrutinized him from head to feet. "And you! Everything I bring up, it's what do we care; it's not our business. I can't avoid what I see, and neither can I dig a hole and bury my curiosity."

"Okay, I'm sorry."

Rolling her eyes, she marched ahead of him.

On December 26th, they woke up at dawn. Their plan was to eat souvlaki for breakfast—her final meal of her favorite Greek food—pizza for lunch at his favorite pizzeria, and at Dunia's invitation, Chinese for dinner. They took pictures in cobble-stoned streets and historical sites, with Parliament's guards and pigeons.

At Dunia's request, Sabah, Kareema and Najieba's family joined them in their farewell tour of Athens. Everyone wore their best clothes and they went to the National Garden where they used up two rolls of film.

At night they walked around Syntagma Square. "I hope the pictures of you turn out alright," Amel said to Dunia.

"My camera's good."

"But if you snap a picture at night, the flash goes through fabric and your underwear shows."

Dunia burst into laughter, and Amel turned red. "It's true," he defended himself. "Everyone knows that."

This brought Dunia to a fit of laughing hysteria and by the time she collected herself, everyone had caught up with them and wanted in on the joke. She swiftly changed the subject.

As they walked further, Amel noticed a song sung in English that shops often played. He liked its melody and asked Dunia what it was about. "That's George Michael," she explained. "He's singing about a man who gave his heart to a girl last Christmas, but the next day she gave it away."

He laughed and hugged her. "That's you."

"I haven't given your heart away."

"Not yet, but the first chance you get, you will."

The table settings, the strange menu, and the prices at the Chinese restaurant made Amel very uncomfortable. Never having had Chinese food before, Dunia had to order for him. When the waiter brought their dinner, Amel complained about the portions. At the Chicken Shack he had suggested they go to, they would have gotten twice as much.

He didn't like the people either. The staff resembled doctors in their white uniforms; the customers were dressed like they were at a wedding. Amel poked fun at them, the egg rolls and chopsticks. "If Sabah was here, he'd have no silver wear to snatch," he said. "These noodles are for worms to eat, not grown men."

"Just eat your food," she said. "You're upsetting my stomach."

"It's not me. It's these green greens."

Amel impatiently drank the oriental tea, anxious for her to charge the bill so they could leave.

She had one thing left to do: bid Amel's neighbors farewell. On the way there, Dunia said "hi" and gave a wide smile to a man sitting on the curb in front of a Christmas shop. Amel pulled her hair. "Who was that?"

"Someone I met," she laughed, looking behind her.

He turned around and saw the man laughing as well.

"Hiii," Amel mocked her with a squeaky voice. "'Hiii,' she says. Could you have been any friendlier than that?"

"I could have, had you given me the chance."

He stared at her rigidly.

"Don't get jealous. I was only nice to him because he gave me the ornament you crushed."

"Is that why you were so attached to it?"

"Absolutely!" She kissed his lips ardently. "Amel, I have a favor to ask. The Lebanese man who helped me find my apartment – I want you to take me to his office. I'd like to say goodbye to him."

"Why must you say goodbye to him?"

"Because he helped me a lot. I don't want to seem unappreciative."

"His place is closed by now."

"Some days he stays open late."

Amel grudgingly took her there. The office door was locked, however. Dunia's disappointment infuriated Amel. "Who is this man for you to give him such great consideration? You don't owe him anything."

"Could you do me a favor?" she asked calmly. "Can you write him a note in Arabic?"

"Dunia!"

"Amel, please. For me?"

Before he could rebuff her, she took a scrap paper and eyeliner out of her purse and told him what to write. "I stopped by to say goodbye, but unfortunately—" Amel stopped writing. "Fine, skip the last word," she said. "But your office was closed. I'm leaving for America. Thanks for everything, Dunia."

Amel's insides churned as she slid the note under the door. They left for Najieba's. Amel stood aside as Dunia kissed each family member goodbye. They gave her their blessings and begged her not to forget to write them.

As silently as treading through a graveyard, Amel and Dunia went around the corner to Kareema's where Dunia repeated the same ritual. This time her tears spilled like blackberries on a cake. Again she received blessings and was asked to correspond.

The tenderest moments of their relationship were on the trolley ride home. They felt the sadness of their approaching separation. They held each other and silently wept, hard enough that they would have flooded the trolley had not their jackets absorbed the tears. Passengers watched, some even cried themselves.

In the apartment, Dunia asked Amel to help her finish packing, but he refused. Unable to watch, he sat in the kitchen. He wrote her a message on a Christmas card: *Dunia, I will never forget you. Faithfully yours, Amel.*

He returned to the messy bedroom. Handing her the card, he asked her not to read it until she arrived in America. He cleared the bed, and while she continued to pack, he lay down and stared at the ceiling.

"Of course, my furniture goes to you," she said. "But I don't want Sabah sleeping on the bed, not ever." Her hands on her waist, she examined her luggage. "I'm leaving you all my shampoo and conditioners. They should last months. These combs too...."

Little by little, her words faded from his consciousness. He closed his eyes. At four o'clock, he felt her lie down beside him. "We have to get up in an hour and a half," she said.

"I know." He stroked her hair and neck. "I love you, Dunia."

"What else?" she whispered.

"I'd die for you."

She nudged closer, then placed her lips over his. "What else?"

"You're my whole life."

"What else?" she asked out of their usual script.

"I worship you."

Smiling, she stopped kissing him. "What did you say?"

"I won't repeat it again," he laughed. "But I meant every word of it."

They got up on time and looked over her apartment. Everything was in order but before they left, Dunia took out three hundred dollars from her pocket and approached Amel. He put up his hand to push away the money. "This is just a loan," she said. "Please, take it."

"Dunia, no. I don't need it."

"Whether you take it or not, it's staying here."

"Let it stay here, but I'm not taking it."

She stared at him lovingly. "Let's not argue. I'm your aunt's daughter. We are family."

He lowered his head as she slipped the money into his hand. They arrived at the airport early and had coffee and pastries while waiting for her flight. Dunia suddenly remembered Amel's gold necklace and tried to remove it.

"No, keep it," he said.

"I can't! Your mother gave it to you."

"You can give it back when we see each other again."

"That might not be for a long time."

"Don't be so sure. Besides, it'll be safer with you."

At 7:40, Dunia wondered if her flight was delayed. "It's supposed to leave at eight and they haven't made any boarding announcement."

She went up to a receptionist who read her ticket. "You are late," she said in Greek. "The plane doors have already closed. Please come this way."

Stunned, Dunia and Amel followed her to an office. The woman murmured something to a husky man seated behind the desk. "Why were you late?" he asked, angrily.

Amel translated to Dunia.

"I wasn't," Dunia said. "I've been here since 6:30."

"Your ticket specifically instructs you to arrive at the airport early."

"Tell him I was early."

Amel did.

"The last bus drove the passengers to the plane ten minutes ago. So you are late!"

After exchanging a few words with the man, the receptionist asked Dunia and Amel to again follow her. She took them to the information desk and asked for Dunia's credit card. Dunia handed it to her and then turned to Amel. "Will they charge a fee or issue me a brand new ticket?" she asked.

"I don't know."

The woman swiped the card and asked Dunia to sign. "Over four hundred dollars spent in one second," Dunia said in a daze. "Because of a stupid mistake."

"For you, no cost is too much," Amel said.

Shaking her head, she faked a smile. Her new flight to Amsterdam was in four hours. Sitting on Amel's lap, she cried all over again. "Don't worry, money comes and goes," he said.

"It's not that. I hate how they treated me. If this were America, I'd demand to speak to a supervisor. How dare they belittle people who visit their country? Where is their professionalism?"

"I'm sorry, Dunia. If I wasn't a refugee, I would've put them in their place."

"It's my fault. I should've realized this isn't Metro Airport. There, the planes leave from the terminal, not five miles away."

"Stop crying," he said, patting her hair. "At least I get to hold you for a few extra hours."

"My parents will think I'm stupid."

"It's better you don't tell them."

"It's on my father's credit card!"

"Make something up."

She snuggled against him. "I'm so tired."

He watched her as she sniffled and relaxed.

"If you decide to marry me," he said before she drifted into sleep, "don't make me wait. Please Dunia, don't make me wait."

She nodded and she dozed off in his arms. Half an hour before boarding Amel woke her up.

"Get ready. This time I'm making sure you're the first to get on the plane."

He watched her check in and walk down a corridor. He called out her name, the sound deep in his throat. She turned and waved, then ushered her long tresses, smart eyes, and tender heart out of his sight. In an instant, he was alone again, and the whole experience seemed as short-lived as a sneeze.

CHAPTER 14

abah tried to persuade Amel to go to a New Year's Eve party at a disco, but was unsuccessful. Kareema's and Najieba's families went to Omonia to celebrate, and begged Amel to join them. He preferred staying home. Around nine o'clock, he fried a frozen hamburger, and he ate while watching TV. He fell asleep before midnight.

New Year's Day, his neighbors stopped by to wish him luck with his visa for America. Sabah came home in the afternoon and told him about the disco. "Girls were amazed by me," he said. "Everyone was dancing funky, so I broke it up by getting in the middle and doing the *depka*."

"By yourself?" Amel asked, looking at the strands of spiked hair around Sabah's bald spot.

"I was teaching them."

Sabah's gold and black vest stood out too, along with his yellow jacket and shiny leopard skin shoes. Amel asked himself how he could tolerate such a clown for a roommate, then remembered it was Sabah who had taken him in. Amel shooed Sabah away and went back to sleep.

He returned to work on January 2nd, rested but heart sore. He missed Dunia beyond words and regretted having encouraged her to leave. Had she lived in Kiffisia, he could have at least visited her on weekends.

"Demitri," his boss shouted. "Demitri, *tilefono.*"

Amel ran to the office. He'd already sent Dunia two letters and called her the night she arrived in Detroit, but his card hadn't lasted long. She had promised to call him at work once the shop reopened.

It was his Aunt Wafaá.

"I visited your aunt's daughter the day after she returned," Wafaá said. "She's a sweet girl. Why didn't you say you had your eyes on her?"

"What would've been the purpose?"

"She could pull you out of Greece."

"I don't want her to think I'm using her to get to America."

"I know that. You love her, right? If she feels the same, she'd want to help."

He was embarrassed. Nobody in America or Iraq knew how uncertain Dunia was about their relationship. "What does Uncle Jabir say?"

"He has already given his blessings," she said. "Once you have Dunia's permission, I'll go to her house and ask for her hand in marriage."

Amel was tongue-tied.

"Your mother spoke with her last night," Wafaá said. "She didn't give an answer, but she was probably too shy. You must speak to her, Amel. She's your fiancée."

Amel borrowed money from a co-worker and after work, called her. Dunia wasn't happy about the spot he, his mother and relatives, had put her in.

"I told you not to say anything," she said. "Now look what's happened. Everyone expects me to know what I want. It makes me look selfish because Amel is sitting on a fire while Dunia is twirling her hair. They're saying you and I are secretly engaged."

"It's my mother's fault. I swear I told her not to mention a word to anyone, but she must've got too excited about her son marrying her favorite niece."

"That's why she got excited?" she asked cynically.

"What do you mean?"

"Why should I be her favorite niece? I've never met her, she's never met me."

"Of course, she'd be happy if I could join my relatives in America too," he added quickly, understanding her implication. "But still, you are her favorite. You're the daughter of her only sister and the love of her oldest son." Amel sighed despairingly. "My time is almost up."

"Call me back collect," she said.

This time, she was softer and wasn't accusatory. "God, I feel so bad, Amel. I feel I'm responsible for your future."

"I'm sorry," he said, for the first time sympathizing with her plight. "I wish I could turn back time and un-notify everyone about us."

"Oh, I don't know what to do," she cried, helpless in a way he wasn't accustomed to from her. "To top it off, my classes are starting in a week. So if I say yes, we'd have to wait until winter break for me to come to Athens and marry you. Otherwise, I'd miss part of school."

"There's a chance that you'll say yes?" he asked, reluctantly.

"One minute I think yes, the next minute, I think no."

"That's not good. These doubts will drive you crazy and hurt your grades once your semester starts."

"I know. Why do you think I'm so upset?"

"Then give an answer and put both our minds to rest."

"I don't have an answer!"

"My relatives are waiting for one."

"I can't give one yet."

"Okay, how much time do you need?"

"A month or two."

"That's too long."

"A month."

"What about a week?"

"Amel, how can I change my whole life in a week?"

"And how can I tolerate another day alone in this godforsaken country? You have no idea what I'm going through."

"How about me?" she said. "My plans were to get my bachelor's degree, then go to law school. Marriage wasn't a consideration. My plans might not seem important to you, but I worked very hard to...." Her speech was suspended as she breathed deeply. "Okay, I will."

"Okay, you will what?" he asked.

"Tell your aunt to come over. We'll talk."

Amel was so happy he was choking on air.

"But don't expect me to move to Arizona," she said.

"Dunia, my future is in Arizona with Uncle Jabir."

"You have lots of relatives here. Your sister in Baghdad just married a guy from Michigan and is moving here soon."

"What do I have to do with my sister and the rest?"

"They're your blood too."

"I have no business ties with them. Uncle Jabir is in charge of my financial situation."

She was quiet.

"Every wife follows her husband," he said. "If I come to Michigan, who'll open doors for me? It'll take us five years to accomplish what we could in six months with my uncle."

"What about my family and school?"

"There are universities in Arizona, as there are in Athens and Michigan. And you can visit your family on weekends."

"It doesn't normally work that way."

"Come on, don't complicate matters. We'll live in Arizona in the beginning and if you can't adjust, in a year or two, we'll move."

"I don't know," she sighed. "I'll have to talk it over with my family."

"Go ahead. They'll agree with what I'm saying."

"And by the way, don't expect children."

"Oh really? Then why do people marry?"

"I don't care why other people marry but as for me, I'm not having kids."

"We'll see," he laughed. "Hey, you haven't told me. Why have you finally said 'yes'?"

"Because the Chaldean guys here suck."

He didn't know which way to take that.

"They're materialistic, judgmental and they like their girls smart but not educated. You're not like that. Maybe war made you humane. Maybe because we're first cousins there's an automatic comfort. Maybe, as corny as it may sound, we really were written for each other."

There was a pause.

"Plus, you're a hard worker," she said. "You'll adjust quickly to America, I'm sure."

Before they hung up, Amel asked if she would send him a copy of that love song they heard while walking on Omonia Street.

"I'll see," she said, annoyed.

"You'll see?"

"I have more important things on my mind, Amel!"

His aunt went to Dunia's house on a Saturday afternoon, but to find out what took place, he had to call Dunia. He woke up his aunt—it was early morning in Athens, late at night in Michigan. He felt foolish for having called collect, but the drachmas he had left were only sufficient for buying onions and potatoes. His next payday was Saturday. He wanted to live off of his earnings rather than exchange the hundred dollar bills she had given him.

His aunt greeted him briefly before she put Dunia on the phone.

"Did Aunt Wafaá come over today?" he asked.

"Yes, she did."

"What's the matter, Dunia? Your voice is different."

"Your Aunt Wafaá isn't what you and your mother describe her to be."

"What did she say?" he asked, concerned.

"She recommended we live with my parents in Michigan."

"What else?" he asked, very worried now.

"Aside from providing us with a grand wedding, she said, they don't want to take on other debts regarding our marriage."

"What were her exact words?" he pressed.

"I'd rather not say."

"Dunia, please. Tell me what she said."

"Basically that your Uncle Jabir's millions have committed suicide. So she wants me to pick up all the expenses."

He was dumbstruck. On such occasions in the Middle East, a girl was approached lavishly with gold and service as a token of her worth. In return, she offered only herself. Any small mishandling from the man's side—stinginess or the wrong word—was disrespectful to her and especially to her family.

"She may be fine with that, but I'm not," he said.

"When she saw how insulted my mom was, she proposed her brother buy roundtrip airline tickets to Athens, a thousand dollar bedroom set, and another thousand for a ring."

Amel was confused. People would pay tens of thousands for a fake marriage to bring a relative to America. Not only were the girls who agreed to it as hard to find as camel meat, but they were usually ugly, divorced or untrustworthy. Some blackmailed the men for life, threatening to turn them in to immigration. Others wanted to bind them to the marriage.

"Then she adds," Dunia said, "'I'm only a messenger. I'll present my brother with the offer. Depending on his financial shape, he may or may not agree.'

"I said to her, 'If your brother is in such a fix, no need to ask him for anything.' So Wafaá reverses her approach and says, 'Jabir has a heart of gold. He might double, even triple the amount.'"

"Had I known this was their view," Amel said, stunned, "I wouldn't have asked you to marry me now."

"She said I'm not a stranger, and there's no shame if my parents help out. But Amel, I'm just a student. As for living with my parents..."

"That's out of the question," he interrupted. His uncle had spent three thousand dollars in souvenirs when he visited Athens. "Provide us with a grand wedding, huh? Anyone can have a grand wedding because people get gifts of money. Tell them they can keep their offer."

"Amel, I wouldn't mind paying. Honest. But their share has nothing to do with my contribution to the marriage," she said gravely. "You being an immigrant, how does she think we'll manage after the wedding? She won't pay our bills or my tuition fees or teach you English or the customs here. She will disappear after the reception and pop up only at family functions."

"Dunia, will you wait for me?" he asked passionately.

"Yes." The word slid into his ears like butter.

"Then we will marry when I get to America."

"But how will you get here?"

"I'll find a way, the same as everyone else."

Amel was breathless when he got home. Sabah looked at him curiously and asked what was the matter.

"Leave me alone," Amel said.

"You want me to make you laugh?"

"No." Amel left the house again, banging the door shut behind him. He walked to the telephone booth and called his Aunt Wafaá to confront her about Dunia. Wafaá told Amel to keep his distance from his maternal aunt's daughter.

"She is not for you," she said. "She doesn't love you, Amel. She specifically said that she only agreed to marry you out of pity."

Amel's mind went blank. He sat in a café and ordered nothing because his pockets were empty. Watching the leaves sway in the wind, he thought he might be better off living in a tree. He might fall off or get hit by lightning, but it wouldn't be his loved ones hurting him.

CHAPTER 15

Amel did or said nothing about the marriage for a week. No one called either. He was expecting to hear from Uncle Jabir or even Uncle Hatim, or Kamil or Faris, but he wasn't hurt when he didn't. There was a lot to sort out; who was telling the truth and why would the others lie?

His mother called one day, weeping. Amel quickly asked to speak to his father, who hid like a ghost in the house until he was required to spook someone. "My uncles made me believe they were dying to get me to America. Now there's an opportunity and suddenly I'm a stranger."

"You don't know the whole story, Amel. One day you'll understand."

Amel wanted to smash the phone. His father had a fit if his mother overcooked dinner but he was calm and collected when his son's nervous system was on the verge of collapsing. He thanked God the line cut off.

Amel's neighbors were aware of what had transpired because he had passed out punch and biscuits when Dunia agreed to marry him. Now they asked about the wedding date and all he could do was shrug. Everyone was considerate, even reveling in his sorrow. Najieba brought him a pot of boiled beets and Kareema made humus. Sabah even cleaned the house and cooked his own special recipe of cauliflower pilaf, made of pork, garlic and chicken wings, but it made Amel sick.

With Sabah's help, Amel rented a truck and moved Dunia's furniture into his house, then turned in her key to the landlord. On Saturday he tossed and turned all night and in the morning he was so tense he couldn't eat breakfast. He knew he had to talk to Dunia, but was too embarrassed to call collect. After getting paid, he could afford a ten-minute conversation.

"Amel, why haven't you called?" Dunia asked as soon as he said hello. "And why aren't you calling collect?"

The tenderness in her voice restored his trust in her and made him suspicious of his aunt. "I spoke to Wafaá."

"Yes, so?"

"Is it true you said the only reason you agreed to marry me was out of pity?" he asked.

"My God, what an instigator! I said no such thing! What a fat liar! The woman stabs you in the back and dances away."

They were momentarily quiet.

"Call me back collect," she said.

He was hesitant, afraid another family member might pick up. Dunia must have read his mind because she promised to answer the phone. When he called back, she continued, "The first time Wafaá came to see me, she brought over a cake and checked me out from head to toe. On her way out, she held my hand tightly, smiled and said, 'May we soon see you as a bride.' Did she think I'm a child, getting me for baked goods and compliments?

"Then, after making Mother and me furious, she comes over a second time, sits on the couch and flips through our pictures from Greece. She comes across the one of us in the airport, and says, 'Amel was so sad. You can see it in his eyes.'

"'He's sad about his situation,' I said. Then she sees a picture of me standing on the balcony in my pink nightgown, which is totally modest. 'Was this taken in his home or yours? Did he take it?' she asks. I knew what she was getting at so I said Kareema's oldest daughter took it. Can you believe what she's implying?"

Amel needed an aspirin. If half of this was true, he didn't want to go to America. His future depended on what his relatives could provide for him. Take that away and all he would have was a sore back.

Dunia's anger didn't cool. She demanded to know why Wafaá had offered nothing but scraps. "Am I defective?" she asked. "I'm not cultured? I have no heritage? And why did Jabir send his sister rather than show up himself? Is he afraid I'm after his money? My family may not be as rich as his, but we're ten times more educated. And we have class. All they have is a Chaldean accent and stores."

Amel felt like he was suffocating. If he hadn't called collect, he might have spared himself this humiliation; now he was stuck listening to insults.

"Do you want to come here through a fiancé visa?" she asked with a softer tone.

"What's that?"

"It's the fastest, cheapest and most secure way to get you here. It sounds too good to be true but it works. I know of two Chaldean couples who have done it. I pay nothing but the application fee and your plane ticket, and in two to three months, you're granted a visa."

"We don't have to be legally married?"

"No. We claim that's our intention. On the forms, we explain our marriage is based on tradition and religion. In our case, it will be easy to convince immigration our engagement is legitimate. We have proof of a long courtship too."

"Then I'll have a green card?"

"That's the catch. In order for you to stay in America, we must get married within ninety days of your arrival."

There was a pause.

"Dunia, do you love me?"

"I don't," she said apologetically. "Isn't it enough I want to marry you?"

"No, it's not."

"Why isn't it? Can't you appreciate my honesty?"

"It's not your honesty I'm after."

"Amel, please. If we have a civil marriage, in private, we'll live separately until we're ready to get married in a church. By then I'll have finished school and you'll have made a life for yourself."

"How many years would we be separated?"

"Well, the law requires three years if you want to keep your green card. Anything after that is up to us, really."

That didn't answer his question. He wanted to know when they could live under one roof. To avoid living with him, he thought, she could probably wait a thousand years. She'd get her law degree, live in Europe, and visit him once every ten years. His presence in her life was as important to her as eating raw eggs.

"What are you thinking?" she asked.

"If I don't enter America with my relatives' support or as your husband, why come?"

"For yourself."

"For myself?" he asked, sourly. Perhaps there was some truth to what Wafaá had said about Dunia pitying him.

"Don't be so sensitive, Amel," she said. "If you love me as you say you do, let me do what would make me happy."

He couldn't give his consent. Whatever way she put it, it felt like charity.

"Now listen carefully," she said as though he had agreed, "I'll need your birth certificate, baptism papers, a copy of your passport and any other important documents."

"I'll send the papers, but I doubt it'll work. If such a visa exists, everyone would have jumped at it."

"It exists. I know more about the system than you do."

Shoving his pride aside, he followed her orders. She picked up the fiancé visa petition from the immigration office then mailed him the forms he had to fill out and sign. With them came instructions she had her mother write in Arabic. Amel came to appreciate her efforts. He bought her ten chocolate bars with hazel nuts, packed them and took them to the post office.

One day he received a letter from Dunia that was more noteworthy (by its weight) than the rest. She had previously written two letters, both beginning with the salutation, *My dear aunt's son, Amel.* While his letters were long, deep, clear, and passionate, hers were short and vague about everything except her plans for school.

Amel suspected that her mother's involvement in writing the letters prevented her from fully expressing herself since Dunia could speak but not write Arabic. Yet a part of him felt Dunia continued the correspondence out of obligation. If he were to end it, she'd simply replace him with a book.

The third letter read:

My dear aunt's son, Amel,

I hope since the last time we spoke you are doing well. As for me, I'm once again confused. Major events lead me to continuously reconsider my role in your life. Wafaá called my mother the other night. She said when Jabir heard of the conflict over money, he was angry. He had tens of thousands to spend on his nephew. Even if he didn't, he'd borrow it—anything to help Amel out of Athens. She asked if we would turn a new leaf and contact Jabir at his place of business.

My mother felt it more appropriate that Jabir call us, but Wafaá said he was a very busy man and convinced her it didn't matter who called who. Now my mother regrets having listened to her. I must admit I'm to blame too. Had I not criticized my mother's old-fashioned mentality, she would've stuck to what she knew to be correct.

Anyhow, your uncle was not polite. He made it clear he had no time for our adolescent behavior. Twice he called us delinquents, making my mother's face turn red. To put an end to the conversation and spare me further degradation, she agreed that you and I break off all communication.

I don't know what Wafaá intended by getting my mother involved. I believe she hates me. I've complicated matters between her and her siblings, and even you, who had a saintly impression of her. Your mother called the other day, crying. She probably thinks my greed is what spoiled your future, not Wafaá's stupidity.

It hurts me to deliver this news to you, given your circumstances, but I have no choice. So far, my father knows nothing. If he finds out, he'll be upset that my mother kept these problems secret. I find myself getting so distracted I can't study. It's too much. I've decided to refocus my attention on my education. I hope this will not influence our relationship. You are my aunt's son, my best friend.

Your aunt's daughter,
Dunia

Amel breathed against the paper. He folded the letter and put it back in the envelope. He wasn't sad that the fiancé visa petition was cancelled. If love wasn't her motive, he wasn't interested.

He himself had researched, through friends and his aunt, the fiancé visa and discovered that once the couple married, immigration relentlessly checked on the applicant and his spouse. If fraud was apparent, Amel could, even with an attorney, get kicked out of the U.S. and Dunia could be fined or jailed. To secure against that, Dunia might suggest they live together a while, and in three years, if they didn't get along, divorce.

But he would never accept such a sacrifice for his sake. He was ashamed of the mess he had created. It had been obvious from the start that Dunia's body, mind and spirit were so unlike his, that matching them together as husband and wife was as unnatural as knitting velvet and feathers into one braid.

CHAPTER 16

on't worry, I won't forget you," sang the young Egyptian singer Omar Idyab.
"Don't worry, no matter who'll call upon me,
I won't live without your eyes.
I won't live with someone else.
You're written in my fate.
My love for you is my passion."

These lyrics played repeatedly in Amel's house. He sent Dunia the cassette tape after she sent the pictures she had taken in Greece. In his initial excitement about finally getting out of Athens, he had forgotten how much Dunia meant to him.

He told his mother he no longer wanted help from his father's side of the family; he would get to America on his own. He started to save. The drachmas he was able to save at the end of the week after he paid bills might eventually get him a ticket to the Greek islands of Mykonos or Santorini, but not America.

His slave wages and Sabah's cheapness and thievery prevented him from saving very much. Since Amel didn't have time, Sabah shopped, then they split the total. One day Amel saw Sabah sitting on the floor through the bedroom window. He was switching prices on the groceries.

Amel wasn't upset. Actually, he thought it humorous and took the opportunity to accuse

Sabah of spending all his money on discos and girls. "You've skipped paying your half of the rent for the past two months," he said. "If I end up putting in the whole fifty dollars next month, one of us has to leave."

Sabah called Amel a backstabber. "After I provided you with a house fancier and bigger than any Iraqi refuge ever lived in, you want me to leave?"

"I don't want you to leave, I want you to contribute your share."

"I won't contribute a toothpick. I have a girlfriend who'll keep me for free."

Amel didn't know whether or not to believe him.

"It's true," Sabah said. "She's from Holland. She wants to marry me."

Amel imagined a worm lying next to a peacock and laughed.

"What's so funny? I'm not lying. The house has four women. All you have to say is 'hi', and they get naked. If you want, come see for yourself."

"What do they do when you say 'bye'?" Amel asked.

"Wave."

Amel was relieved Sabah moved out quietly, taking only the TV and stereo. He at once searched for another roommate. There were plenty to pick from but he wanted someone decent, and not related. Kareema and Hakeem asked him if they could trade homes.

"Your house is a quarter the size of mine, yet the same rent," Amel said. "It doesn't have a kitchen or shower."

"You can use the kitchen and shower whenever you want," Kareema said. "We'll live in your house, but it'll stay yours. You can ask for it back when you please."

Amel declined. True, one person didn't need space for ten, but at a time when he had nothing else going for him, his comfort was a necessity. Without funding from his uncles or a visa from the U.S. embassy, Athens might become his permanent home.

A few weeks later, Amel was staining a mahogany desk and looking forward to lunch when his boss called him into his office. He gave him a big speech about how much he liked and cared for him, then fired him. Business was slow lately, jobs in the furniture shop had to be eliminated. He asked Amel to finish the day's work and pick up his wages.

The sound of machinery changed to a turbulence of questions and panic as Amel blankly returned to the mahogany desk. He raised the paintbrush and dipped it in the can. Unable to snap out of his shock, he wished Sabah were there to tell a joke.

During the bus ride home, he stared at the passengers. A woman smiled at him and he wondered why people had bad teeth. There were dentists on every corner. All they needed was to make an appointment and pay a fee. Maybe they didn't care their teeth were rotting.

How stupid everyone on the bus was, including the driver. He drove so fast the bus swayed, nearly tipping over. Then the bus broke down and the driver asked for men to help push. Amel wouldn't budge: never again would he aid an Athenian in distress! Let the bus get swallowed by a pothole! Let the world puke! But soon he was out on the street, the rear of the bus pushed against his nose.

On the way home, he saw a cat run towards an injured bird. Amel hurriedly crossed to intercept. He picked up the bird, hid it in bushes, then left the scene feeling exhilarated. Every problem had a solution, he thought. Amel could be less particular about whom to take in as a roommate until he found a job. He could live off the money Dunia had given him.

Amel was unemployed for a month, which he spent listening to sad Arabic and Greek songs on a cassette player he had borrowed from Kareema and eating frugal dinners of fried potatoes or bread and butter. Sometimes Najieba brought over a cup of rice pilaf. Kareema and Hakeem often invited him for cocoa. One day, he was hired by Sabah's previous employer at the picture frame shop, where he made more money than before and put in fewer hours.

He also found a new roommate, Hussam, introduced to him by Najieba's husband. Hussam was an educated and quiet Chaldean man, spending most of his free time reading the Koran. "I like to be familiar with all world religions," was his excuse to Amel.

Sabah said Hussam was in love with a Muslim. That, not the war, was the primary reason he had left Baghdad. To safeguard his family's reputation and spare the girl's feelings, he wanted to move to America and forget her. The opposite proved to be true when he bought himself the Koran.

By spring, Amel had accepted his situation. He befriended the stray cats of the neighborhood by leaving out a bowl of milk or leftovers on the windowsill. Knowing he could never save enough money to get into America, he envisioned a color television set and stereo system instead. Hussam agreed to pitch in.

Things were going well until a letter arrived from Dunia. He hadn't heard from her in months, and she wasn't one to write unless there was something important to say. He opened the letter, half excited, half afraid.

Amel didn't like the tone of the letter. She began with, *My dear brother Amel.* His romantic status dropped back a few notches. If his curiosity hadn't pressed him to continue, he would have skipped the rest and listened to Greek music. He started over.

My dear brother Amel,

It has been a long time since our last contact. I hope you've been in good health. I'm fine. Everything is as usual. I'm writing to you without my mother's assistance. My aunt has agreed to help me instead. Although my parents didn't forbid me to speak to you, I don't want to involve them.

As I'm sure you know, your sister Neherein arrived in Michigan last week. Her in-laws held a welcoming party for her and we were invited. At first, I didn't want to attend with my parents, but I went so your relatives wouldn't think I'm holding a grudge.

I mean no disrespect, Amel, but I must say your relatives have no manners. We weren't received rudely by your Aunt Wafaá, but your Uncle Hekmat was very distant. After that, no one spoke to us. They simply watched us with hostile eyes.

The next day Wafaá called, again wanting to explain her side of the story. I think she feels guilty that her interference kept you in Athens. Now she blames your mother for ruining our chance together. Supposedly, your mother said, before Wafaá came to see us, that I didn't want a thing and took full obligations for the marriage expenses.

That was what threw Wafaá off. By the time Jabir heard that wasn't the case and volunteered to help, your parents said no, 'no, thank you'. He was hurt. That was his reason for being harsh towards my mother.

Wafaá asked my mother to privately reopen the subject with your sister. My mother refused, but Wafaá reminded her she's your aunt too and regardless of the past, she should help you. With my permission and since we had to take a house warming gift to your sister, we agreed to Wafaá's plan.

When we arrived at Neherein's house, Wafaá was there. We had brunch, then Wafaá excused herself to pick up her son from school. As directed by Wafaá, my mother asked Neherein questions about you, your parents, the proposal, etc. But Neherein said she knew nothing and we left your sister's house, astounded.

My mother called Wafaá that night and angrily asked what was the meaning of this circus? Why were we being stretched like bubble gum in front everyone? Wafaá apologized for your sister's behavior, calling her own niece a cow and an airhead. Personally, I think Wafaá has a vendetta against me.

I know you're not responsible for your aunt's actions, but please see she somehow stays out of my business. Her meddling costs me sleep and is affecting my grades. I'm sorry to ask you to do this during your difficulties, but to avoid a family feud, I feel I must.

Take good care of yourself, and give my regards to Kareema, Najieba and their families.

Your friend,
Dunia

Amel felt foolish. When he had proposed, he had, thanks to his relatives in America, overestimated his financial and social position. He switched off whatever images he once thought were true and zoomed into the reality that he would forever be a struggling refugee.

CHAPTER 17

In early September, Amel sat on his windowsill and threw pita bread at the cats as he listened to the rustle of dry leaves in the wind. It sounded similar to rain, but it was sunny.

Amel had been living among strangers so long that he had stopped feeling like a stranger himself. The inner voice that told him to return to Iraq had subsided. He still missed Baghdad's vendors call— "Hot and spicy pickled mangos! Thick and tasty goat's yogurt! Freshly squeezed orange, pomegranate, banana juice"—but he knew he would not, could not go back.

He envisioned Dalaal's Bakery where he had bought bread every morning, the women's veils flirting with the wind, his mother holding a jug of water, his sisters' braids swinging to and fro. He wished he could hold Baghdad's dust in his palms and inhale it like flower petals one last time.

He petted his favorite cat, the one with lime eyes and cream and brick hair. She dropped by more frequently than the others. She was like Dunia, getting what she needed, then disappearing. Amel's mind attempted to tiptoe away from Dunia. He had to start using common sense.

While Dunia would be his first and last love, he had been nothing more to her than a borrowed car, steering him north, south, east, west, stopping at her convenience, starting when she felt like it, loading him up with her moodiness and tantrums and, at the end of the ride, forgetting to unload.

She hadn't gone to the islands as she had claimed. Amel discovered hardly anyone visited the islands in the winter, as many facilities were closed. Then where had she gone, he wondered, and with whom? A classmate maybe or she had met someone and taken up his offer of a souvlaki sandwich!

He remembered how casually she had lied and he was curious to know where she had gone on days when she showed up hours late. Unable to bear the mental image, he piloted towards another complaint—she was completely self-centered. If he had a chance to rest, she would drag him to ancient ruins of broken rocks and pornographic statues.

For every compliment he gave, he received a demand. They would be walking along and Dunia would point at a girl's bag of potato chips and say, "I want that!" She would see a yogurt commercial on TV and say, "Let's have that for breakfast tomorrow!" Like a dog with a dangling tongue, he would fetch whatever she desired.

And if he made the mistake of being too affectionate, he was removed like the fat on a steak. If he were ever again lucky to touch a steak, he wouldn't remove the fat. He would roll it in bread with parsley and chow it down. Then he would lick the juice off the plate. Same with chicken skin. The best parts of meat and poultry grossed Dunia out. His family would sympathize with his cravings. They deep fried *kufta* or chicken wings on weekend nights and ate them like popcorn.

He heard Hussam dragging his sandals. "Amel, do you want two or three eggs for breakfast?"

"Three," Amel said, and recalled Dunia telling him the one thing he was good at was cooking eggs.

Damn that Satan, had she not been a liar! He cursed, despite himself. He wished he had never met her, that she would die so he would stop thinking about her. Shaking his head, he went into the kitchen and slurped the eggs as if they were milk.

As Christmas approached, Amel built picture frames for his family. He also dug into his savings and bought his mother and oldest sister paintings, partially engraved in gold, of Jesus Christ and the Virgin Mary. He mailed the packages in November to ensure they arrived on time.

Dunia wasn't on his Christmas list because he had already sent her a picture frame for her birthday, along with a card of a little naked girl with angel wings holding up a red heart-shaped pillow. The girl's innocence and tousled hair resembled Dunia so much that he had kissed the card prior to mailing it.

Dunia hadn't called or written to thank him. Amel swore never again to send her anything, not even a candy wrapper. Had her heart beat at the sound of his voice, she would have called. If any romantic feelings existed, she wouldn't have addressed him in letters as a brother.

He was dwelling on Dunia's faults when he heard Najieba's family had been granted a visa to America. That was always bittersweet news for refugees to hear. While rejoicing, they couldn't block the pangs of envy. Months back, Shams and her family had been granted a visa to Canada.

Najieba divided her furniture and kitchenware among her friends. Amel got a large pot, a few recipes and a warning about lettuce and other greens, "Store them unwashed, in a perforated vegetable bag, away from fruits. Don't serve before you wash them in very cold water and spin them dry."

Amel knew Najieba meant well, yet he wanted to choke her. He hated his life more than ever. He imagined Sabah, Hussam, Shams and Kareema's families—one by one—plucked out of Athens by a helicopter while he waved goodbye. His lifelong career would then be to welcome incoming refugees. He could bang his head against the wall of the American Embassy and they wouldn't grant him so much as a Band-Aid.

One uplifting event that happened shortly after Christmas was that his sister in America had a baby boy. He was amazed at how proud he felt, considering how much Neherein irritated him. Her only interests had been marriage and money. Other relationships or objectives didn't count. Aunt Wafaá had rightfully called her a cow and an airhead.

Long periods of separation from family wised up a person, he theorized. Her new role as a mother would surely have an improving effect too. Now that he was an uncle, he wanted to provide his nephew with a grand baptism gift, but he could afford something mediocre at best. He brooded over what to do and came up with a lavish and loving present—the necklace Dunia was safeguarding.

Initially acquired by his mother, the gold necklace had the Aboona imprint. Passing it on to his sister's son would strengthen family connections, be witnessed by cheering relatives, and video taped. He was ecstatic to be involved with his family again in such an impressive way.

Amel called to congratulate Neherein and boast about the gift. Her gleeful laugh and the baby's cries in the background proved he had made the right choice. But he had one favor to ask his sister. "Can you relay the message about the necklace to Dunia? We haven't spoken for so long, it'd be odd to call her out of nowhere. Plus, I can't afford it."

"Why does she have your necklace?"

"She's keeping it safe," he explained, uncomfortably. "I asked her to."

The instant he hung up, he felt a bump in his plan that had seemed smooth as custard. Not anymore. He couldn't pinpoint where the bump was, but five days later, it got bigger.

On December 22nd he received a large package by registered mail. He noticed Dunia's name as he signed for it. He opened the box in confusion. Inside were presents and a Christmas card which greeted everyone, acknowledged Najieba's departure from Athens, and included instructions for dispensing the gifts. Each of Kareema's daughters got a Barbie, hair accessories, crayons and nail polish. Amel got cologne and aftershave in a sport's bag.

Amel notified the neighbors of their gifts. After the girls, screaming, picked up their dolls and left, he lay in bed, remembering disturbing details about the necklace. In her letters, Dunia had mentioned she wore it night and day, not removing it even to shower.

What an imbecile he was! The necklace had sentimental value for her, and he had treated it like a disposable razor. By now, she had been told to give it back. He wondered what her opinion of him was in the wake of such mind-boggling immaturity.

One day, he received a small envelope with Dunia's return address but no name. She'd written a brief note, with no salutation, on an index card. It read:

> *Wafaá called weeks ago and asked that I give her your necklace. I delivered it, along with the coat you had me keep, to your sister. Rest assured that the matter is now resolved. By the way, I sent you a package on December 14th, which I fear has been lost. Our post office said you need to check with the Athens post office. The mailman might have come when you weren't home.*

She didn't sign her name. He placed the index card in the envelope and tucked it in a shoebox with her letters, pictures and other things he had collected—dental floss, bobby pins, rubber bands, pencils and the yellow thread—that she had left in her apartment.

A few weeks later, his boss called him to the office. "Demitri, *tilefono*," she said, handing him the receiver.

"Hello," Amel said.

"Did you get my letter?" It was Dunia.

"Yes," he said hoarsely.

"Have you checked at the post office like I told you?"

"The package arrived."

"It arrived?" she exclaimed. "When?"

"A few days before Christmas. Did you receive the frame I sent for your birthday?"

"Amel, why didn't you tell me you got the package?"

"I didn't know you would think it was lost."

"Did you get my note?"

"Yes."

"And you didn't call?" She laughed, sarcastically. "Here I am, thinking you moved."

"Where would I go?"

"I don't know. I just figured when a person doesn't reply, they're not there."

"How are your classes?" he asked.

"They're good. I start law school in the fall."

"Congratulations."

There was a silence between them like a drum. It amplified his idiocy. He wanted to say he was sorry and ask her to forgive him, but would she?

"And yourself, Amel?" she asked. "What are your plans?"

"I have none."

"Why not? You can't stay in Athens forever."

"Where would I go?"

"To America, where else?"

"Why would I want to go there now?"

"For your sister, your nephew, aunts and uncles," she said with cynicism.

"I'm fine here, thank you."

Once again silence, tolerable since he had been abused.

"Tell me what options one has to get to America," she said.

"None."

"Amel, please. Work with me. What options are there?"

"I said none."

"Don't be stubborn!" she demanded. "Not about this subject."

"What do you care?"

"I do care. I want you to be with your family."

"My family is in Iraq."

"Amel, what are the options?" she pressed.

"Through Canada."

"How?"

"There's a smuggler with stolen and bought passports, some U.S., others European. He escorts you to the airport and gets you on a plane to Canada. When you land, you ask for political asylum. Later, you find your own way to cross the border to Detroit."

"What does he charge?"

"Five thousand dollars."

She was quiet a while. "Tonight you'll call your uncle and ask him for the money."

"I will never ask my uncle for another thing."

"Don't complicate matters. You know if you ask, he'll give it to you."

"If that was true, why hasn't he offered? He knows I want to get out."

"After the misunderstandings, he doesn't know you want him to help."

He sighed heavily.

"Are you on speaking terms?"

"No. I only talk with my immediate family."

"How stupid! Do you think your uncle has nothing better to do than read your mind and think of ways to get you to America?"

He sighed a heavier sigh.

"Regardless of what happened, Amel, he's your uncle and your only way out."

"I will not lower myself."

"There's no stooping with blood relations. Besides, it was mostly your fault. You shouldn't have opened your mouth about marriage before getting his permission. If he was your sponsor, he should've been consulted first."

He was speechless. Her efforts, woven with color and care, embroidered by science and softness, touched him like warm rain.

"I'm going to call you tomorrow to find out what happened," she said. "So you'd better have spoken to him by then."

Amel smiled to himself. So what if she had lied in the past? His relatives in America were liars too. They gave a false image of their wealth and generosity and made him look like a donkey. Still, Dunia was right. Those weren't adequate reasons to steer away from America. Alone in Athens, he'd rot.

Besides, more than ever, his family counted on him to help them out of Baghdad. He had been so involved in loving Dunia and survival, he had forgotten that their dreams and hopes were fastened to his. Amel shifted his heart and dialed his uncle's telephone number.

CHAPTER 18

The phone rings were frightening. They dragged on like stairs that spiraled upwards forever. One of his uncle's cashiers answered and put him on hold. Amel kept calm by focusing on the empty café across the street, its blue cushioned chairs flipped over on white tables as a man in an apron swept the floor.

When his uncle said 'hello', Amel was momentarily deaf to everything but his own quivering voice. Their greeting was so formal that the space for Amel to make requests narrowed from yarn to string size. The meter ran like a hungry leopard.

"Have there been any changes since we last spoke?" his uncle finally inserted.

"I'm working in a picture frame shop now."

"I heard. I meant in regards to your refugee status."

"It's the same," Amel said, hoping his uncle would get to the point faster and friendlier.

"Hmmm."

Amel had eighty seconds to go. "Uncle, there's a new route people are taking to get to America. It's through Canada."

"I've heard about it. What are the specifics?"

"Ah, my card is almost up...."

"Why didn't you call collect?" he asked knowingly.

Amel didn't answer.

"Call me back collect, got it?"

Amel was relieved. He had just enough drachmas on his card to call the AT&T operator. The second conversation had instant familiarity. Amel told his uncle the details of the plan, but avoided mentioning the costs.

"How much does the smuggler want?" his uncle asked.

"Five thousand."

"Five thousand, hmmm?" Uncle Jabir sighed. "Why so expensive? I've heard that others made it in with three thousand. Have you shopped around, bargained?"

"The guy I'm telling you about has a success rate of a hundred percent. So far no refugee who hired him was caught and sent back."

"How long has he been in business?"

"I'm not sure. No one knows much about his background. Even his name is a mystery."

"Do more research, Amel. Compare prices. There's lots of fraud in the world."

"I will," Amel said, disappointed by his uncle's lack of enthusiasm.

Amel walked with his head hanging and his hands in his pockets. Make him a business partner—right! A billion stores already in his name, very funny! The only job his uncle had for him was clipping nose hairs. His relatives' descriptions of America were the real fraud, home theaters and 24-hour pharmacies. What fabrications.

Dunia called him the following day.
"Did you talk to your uncle?" she asked.
"Yes."
"What did he say?"

"He asked why it is so expensive. Some other guy made it to Canada for three thousand."

"Is that all?" she laughed. "The way you sound, I thought he rejected you."

"No, but he makes a fuss over a two thousand dollar difference when he has millions?"

"Amel, it doesn't matter. You mustn't be so sensitive. So your uncle is a tightwad. So what? Just get the damn money and get out. Later today, call the smuggler...."

"No, not now."

"Yes, now!"

"I don't have his number."

"Get it."

"It's too early. I'm not ready."

"What's wrong with you?" she asked, peeved. "Sooner or later, you'll have to leave Athens. If you keep stalling, you could lose the Canada option."

His reply was not a 'yes', but she responded as if it was.

"I'll call in a few days to see what happened," she said. "You better not screw this up."

Amel was touched. She had once again coached him towards his goal. He returned to the ebony frame he was gluing together. It was for a landscape, where the trees looked like stacked green parasols and the bunched flowers like cotton candy.

He put the frame aside to dry and grabbed the next one, made of oak. How terrific Dunia was, he thought. Before, she was the love of his life, now he saw the lawyer side. The depth of her education, along with her beauty and confidence, made him wonder why she bothered with a pigeon like him. Did she feel obligated? He dwelled on the possible reasons, knowing she didn't do it out of love.

Getting the smuggler's number was a headache. He was sent from one person to another. When he finally called, the wife said her husband, Dion, was away on business. She didn't know if he was coming back tomorrow or next week. Friends told Amel the police might have arrested him.

Almost relieved, Amel decided to forget about smuggling. Dunia and her smart ideas! She was like a car without brakes; a television set that wouldn't turn off. Poor girl, the older she got, the more her condition worsened.

"Is what you heard factual or a rumor?" Dunia asked after he related his scant information.

"I don't know."

"Did you read it in a newspaper, hear it on the radio, watch it on television? Did you visit him in prison, or what?"

"Some guy told me."

"So it's a rumor?"

"I don't know," he said, feeling that his intellect, in contrast to hers, was made out of thin air.

"I don't believe rumors, Amel. Tomorrow, you call again."

"It's not safe. The guy is probably in jail, anyway. Why else would his wife be so vague?"

"Don't be stupid. His wife protects him."

"Why are you pushing me, Dunia?" he asked, overwhelmed by her effort.

"I don't want you to spend the rest of your life stranded in Athens."

Her kindness propelled him to speak. "Dunia, I want to talk to you."

"So talk."

He took a deep breath. "I know I've done stupid things. But I never once stopped loving you.

After you left Athens, my love grew stronger. I don't know how that was possible, since I thought I couldn't love you anymore than I already did.

"I know you didn't feel the same. In America, I'm sure you felt the exact opposite. You were angry with me, maybe even hated me, and I don't blame you. But what hurt me like nothing ever has, what I will never forget is how you lied. You didn't go to the islands with your class, Dunia. You went somewhere else, with a person—I don't know who."

There was momentary silence.

"This is what you wanted to talk to me about?" she asked in disgust. "You wait a year and choose this moment to bring up the past? You never were able to get it right. You either pushed too hard or withdrew completely. Both ways hurt me."

She laughed with sarcasm. "You're no different today," she said. "You tell me you love me and accuse me of lying in one breath. I have no intention of getting into this with you on the phone. What brought this on now, Amel, when I've put my personal issues aside in an attempt to help you?"

She hung up without saying goodbye. Amel was dumbstruck. He asked his boss if he could go home, and once home, he vomited. Hussam offered medicine, but he refused it and went to bed. He didn't get up until Sabah stopped by in the evening, along with Kareema's daughters.

"Leave," Sabah said to the girls. "I have a dirty joke to tell."

"Like we've never heard dirty jokes," Manal said, swinging her hips.

"Yeah, like we never have," Maram mimicked.

"You little devils, get out of here!"

"You can't kick us out," Maysoon said. "It's not your house anymore."

"What a disrespectful monster you've turned into," Sabah said, thumping her head. "And I thought you were the most decent of the three."

She stuck her tongue out as he shooed them outside. Sabah saw Amel and asked Hussam, "What's the matter with him?"

"He's sick."

"What's he sick about? I heard he's getting out through Canada."

"I guess the guy's in jail."

"No!" Sabah's eyes widened and his mouth dropped.

"They say police have been after him a while now."

"Wow! Anyway, listen to this joke. A nun and priest are riding a camel..."

"Who's driving?" Hussam asked.

"The priest is driving. The camel dies and they're alone in the desert. They're bored, so the nun asks the priest if she could show him something he hadn't seen before. He says, 'I never saw a woman naked.' She takes off all her clothes and he points to her thing and asks, 'What's that?' She says, 'That's where babies come from.' So now the priest asks if he could show the nun something she hadn't seen before. She says, 'I never saw a man naked.' He takes off his robe and she asks, 'What's that?' He says, 'That's what gives life.' She says, 'Then why don't you stick it in the camel so he can get up and get us the hell out of here?'"

Hussam asked Amel why he wasn't laughing.

"Because he's a silly idiot who doesn't know how to be happy," Sabah said. "I have another one! A man and a woman are making out, right? The guy has his hand down there and the girl says, 'Ouch, your ring is hurting me.' He says, 'That's not my ring. It's my watch.'"

The next day Amel's condition wasn't much better, but he went to work. Head pounding, stomach turning, he feared he would jab a nail through his hands rather than the wood. His co-workers made the situation worse by continuously asking if he was all right. He was relieved that Dunia called him at the end of the week.

"The other day I heard your side of the story," she said. "Now listen to mine. You always assume I don't have feelings for you but that's not true. Mine just weren't as strong as yours were for me. They never had a chance to develop. From the start, I resisted you. I wasn't ready to be involved in a serious relationship, particularly not one overseas.

"Still, partly against my will, you brought us together and later, totally against my wishes, you made our courtship public. I know there's no comparison between my problems and yours, but for what it's worth, imagine me coming home after three months—I haven't yet unpacked—and I'm asked to say 'yes' or 'no' to a crucial question. Then I'm subjected to Wafaá's despicable games.

"Aside from my parents, no one took into account that my future was at stake. And your position along the way? First you desert me and later you put your sister ahead of me. The day Wafaá said you wanted the necklace for your nephew, I thought she was lying. You broke our pact and made me look bad."

Someone was calling him, and he yelled at them to give him a few more minutes. Then he asked her to continue.

"As for the lie, I was trying to spare you pain. I didn't get away just because of a guy, but also to get away from you. You had so much hope for us and I didn't want to lead you on. Now I know we don't belong together. Never. Still, you're my aunt's son. I want us to be friends. Do you respect that?"

"Yes."

"Good. Stay on top of the Canada route, and...."

"Forget about that," he interrupted. "Forget about Canada. America means nothing to me now."

"You're being ridiculous again. Don't make me the cause of your unhappiness. Please, don't make me feel guilty."

He was quiet.

"Come here, Amel, you hear me? I won't forgive you or myself if you don't."

Amel met Dion at a café on Fokionos Negri Street. Dion was a thin man with large eyes and a pulpy nose that scrutinized and sniffed Amel from top to bottom like a trained pit bull. A cigarette in his hand, he drank Greek coffee and gave Amel brief instructions.

"Have the money ready, okay?" he said. "It'll stay in your possession until the day of departure, which will be any day within the next couple of weeks."

The waiter approached their table. Amel ordered a cappuccino.

"How will I know when?" Amel asked.

"You won't. Do you have the money?"

"My uncle will wire it to me."

Dion handed him his napkin and a pen. "Write your full name and address." Amel did so.

"As soon as there's the right passport and a flight is available, you'll hear from me, okay?"

"How will I prepare—my job, roommate?"

"You won't. This is not land smuggling, it's a plane."

"I've never been on a plane before."

Dion pressed his cigarette in the astray. "It works like this, okay? You go to work, visit friends, everything normal. Don't say goodbye to anyone or start selling your furniture. It will raise suspicions."

"I don't need to learn some English?"

"The men at the checkpoint will let you pass, don't worry. I recommend that once you're in Canada, pretend you know no English. Then contact your relatives quick. Get an attorney." He viewed him side to side. "Try to have stubbles and keep your hair very short."

Amel nodded.

The man finished his coffee, searched his pocket for change and placed forty-three drachmas on the table. "I'll see you later."

He disappeared into the crowd.

Once the money arrived, Amel sat patiently as a chicken over its eggs. Eight days passed. At 4:00am on Wednesday, he heard loud knocking. Fear and excitement had been keeping him from sleeping well so it didn't take long to answer his door.

"We're leaving now," Dion said, rubbing his hands together to keep warm. "Bring nothing but a carry-on."

Half in shock, Amel turned around to go back inside, when Dion added, "Do you have a sports cap?"

"I think so."

"Wear it."

Hussam woke up and watched Amel dress and pack. He was the only person who bid him farewell. They embraced. "Good luck," Hussam said.

In the car, Dion offered Amel gum. "Chew like a Westerner, not a cow, okay?" he said. "Walk like nothing is a big deal." He gave him an Irish passport and the airline ticket. "This is your flight number. You'll land in Toronto, okay?"

Amel opened the passport to look at the picture. The resemblance wasn't close, but he kept his mouth shut. He was dropped off at the airport.

"I'll wait until the flight leaves," Dion said. "An ugly man with a gold pen in his hand will help you board. He'll gesture for you to stand in his line. Pay attention, okay?"

Amel practiced breathing as he went inside. He slipped through the first counter like butter. At the terminal, an airline employee turned and glared at him, the rage so unsettling that Amel moved away from his vision. Then he realized that was his ally. The man checked his passport and let him through.

In the shuttle bus, Amel was amazed at his own composure. Staring at the buildings and lights behind him, he wondered if this was real. He knew he was in an altered state of consciousness.

He made it inside the plane, his legs trembling as he sat down. He felt equal parts joy and pain. The plane began to taxi. He focused on the no smoking and seatbelt signs. His energy rose with the massive acceleration of take-off, his heart beating hard as everything else moved very slowly.

Observing the buildings and cars below shrink to toy-size, he was in a twofold reality, a spider clinging to its web as a child's fingertips pulled it away.

Once they were flying, an unnatural act for humans, he slept from weariness. He dreamed of a ceremony where everyone he knew, dead and alive, came forth to congratulate him. When he opened his eyes, clouds danced in the sky as if in sacred ritual. He felt like God's guest looking at the universe.

When the captain announced they would be landing shortly, his apprehension began all over again. Amel went to the lavatory and as Dion had instructed, tore up the passport and flushed it down the toilet. When they landed, he felt refreshed. The intense energy from the flight dissipated.

Time moved quickly now. People's speech was unintelligible and their activities accelerated. His thought process became so fragmented it caused visual and auditory distortions, but grasping the truth of his convictions, he pulled himself together and approached customs. He asked for political asylum.

CHAPTER 19

esterday he was there, now he was here. He had been living in an eerie theater for years, and he had survived, unscathed. An inner voice kept jumping up to say, "What in God's name is going on?" Once immigration officials released him to his uncle Basam, he had no idea what people were saying or doing—they talked gibberish and milled around aimlessly.

As soon as he arrived at Cousin Shams' house, he showered and took a nap, dreaming he was on the wing of an airplane, flying over a desert at night.

Amel stayed at Shams' while Aunt Wafaá and Uncle Basam arranged for him to live in Windsor. He was looking forward to living an hour away from Dunia and his relatives. Shams' home was bearable even though her stinginess had gotten worse. Now she watched how much sugar he used in his tea.

He was too busy to care. With his relatives he planned his future. Uncle Basam hired an attorney, Aunt Wafaá looked for an apartment, and Uncle Jabir called several times to discuss how to get him into the U.S.

He was impatient to get things moving. He knew he couldn't walk straight into America, shake hands with the president, and ask for a job at the White House. But the last thing he wanted was to waste time sitting in a home that kept track of his sugar intake.

Dunia called the fifth day he was in Toronto.

"I just heard last night," she said tenderly. "I'm so happy for you, Amel."

"Thank you."

"Was it frightening?"

"I'd have to say yes."

"I'm so happy for you."

"Thank you."

"Were you hassled?"

"At the Toronto airport. They interviewed me for hours, until my uncle showed up," he said. "He flew in from Detroit."

"Do you plan to stay at Shams'?"

"No. I'll be living in Windsor soon."

"I figured that. Make sure you call once you move, so my parents and I can visit."

"Why are you bringing your parents along?"

"My mother is your aunt, isn't she?"

"Oh yes, of course," he said, embarrassed.

"Let me give you my work number in case you don't find anyone home."

"When did you start working?"

"Last summer. I was hired part-time at a law office."

"A law office!" he said, impressed. "Can they help me get into the U.S. legally?"

"It's not immigration law. It's litigation. They sue people."

Amel wondered how he would ever match her résumé. While hers had many refinements and rankings scribbled on it, his had two: Iraqi refugee and woodworker.

The apartment complex in Windsor faced a main street and was old and dirty. The apartment itself was renovated and clean and his furniture, kitchenware and appliances were collected by Wafaá from various family members. Wafaá also stocked his medicine cabinet and filled his refrigerator with produce, Arabic cuisine, sweets and pastries.

Dunia and her parents performed their duty by bringing him a tray of baklava one afternoon. Amel's sister was there to help serve brunch and wash dishes. Dunia had put on a few pounds and was dressed modestly, in long ivory pants and a loose yellow sweater. Her eyes were as firm as ever and her hair, scrunched together like asparagus, had grown thicker.

She had inherited a lot of her traits from her father Boutrus, Amel realized: his intelligent eyes and crooked nose, his height and confidence. Boutrus sat like a king at ease. He entered their discussion once, to reveal a fact—about a politician or a recently endorsed law—that informed readers and news watchers would be aware of.

Dunia's mother was the same as Amel remembered her from Baghdad: short, heavy around the hips and stomach, homely and kind. She wore a brown dress with black wild cats running upwards. Dunia must have bought it for her for Christmas.

"Neherein, how have you been?" Aunt Moneera asked when the room got uncomfortably quiet.

Neherein ate watermelon seeds as if they were nuts. "Fine, fine, we thank God."

"And Amel, what are your plans now?"

Amel explained what his uncle was plotting for him.

"Your father made a big mistake not to wait for his green card," Boutrus said to Amel. "The whole family could have been here by now."

Amel saw where Dunia's bluntness came from.

"True, but what can you do?" Amel had a hard time talking as he wondered how much Boutrus knew of what occurred between Dunia and his relatives.

"Everyone advised him to get his green card first," Boutrus persisted. "But he said no—as if the card was a worm that would eat his rear pocket."

Amel broke into a sweat.

"If everyone carried the past on their shoulders, no one would stand up straight," Aunt Moneera rescued her nephew.

Boutrus shrugged and drank his tea. "Nothing is wrong with addressing what has happened." He turned to Amel. "I knew your father's thoughts of America back then. So much freedom scared him. But he should have used his head not his emotions to make such an important decision."

Boutrus was such a duplicate of Dunia that Amel lowered his gaze. Having had the last word, the next subject Boutrus opened was about the sanctions against Iraq and Saddam's strategies, as though, Amel thought, he was Saddam's right-hand *wazir* when he hadn't set foot in Baghdad for over thirty years. He even made a few weird comments about mountains and oxygen.

The visit lasted two and a half hours and felt longer. Despite the politeness and conversation, there was too much tension as he and Dunia had avoided all eye contact. She barely spoke and busied herself with eating *kinafé*. He was glad when it ended.

He called Dunia at their appointed time, between 11:00pm and 11:30pm, and asked what she thought of his apartment. "It's nice, isn't it?" he said before she could answer. "When can you visit on your own?"

"I don't think that's a good idea," she said. "Your aunt or sister might stop by."

"This is not Baghdad or Athens. No one shows up without calling first."

"You've been in Windsor less than a month, and you're not working. You're not that important yet. Family and friends don't have a set routine with you."

Amel didn't try to convince her otherwise, knowing he wouldn't succeed. However, he invited her over again the next day. She gave the identical answer. He did not, could not, give up. He was bored to death. Even his shadow was lonely in the one bedroom apartment.

The neighbors never said 'hello', his relatives had a million and one reasons why they couldn't visit, nothing happened on his street. He wasn't permitted to work, but he was eligible for classes. English as a second language met Tuesday and Thursday mornings. He attended with twelve Iraqis, two Chinese, one Portuguese, and one Mexican. Amel befriended a few of the Iraqis, but they bored him. They were nothing compared to Sabah, Kareema's and Najieba's families, and Hussam. He missed his old friends.

"At least you're learning," Dunia said when he complained.

"Someone told me the teachers are so dumb they even give certificates to those who don't attend."

"They're trying to encourage the students."

"They're idiots."

A few days later, Dunia called him. She mentioned her family was at a gathering and she had been studying all day for a test. She was fed up with comprehensions and analytical reasonings and wanted to get away. "Can I come over?" she asked.

He tried to curb his enthusiasm, but still it spilled over. "Yes, come over!"

"Don't expect me to come inside," she warned. "I'll beep my horn. Look for me from the window or sit outside."

"It's cold."

"Don't be a baby."

He took his camera and a Pepsi while waiting on the front steps, checking out each vehicle from afar. He spotted Dunia's hair at the traffic light. Amel watched her park her champagne colored Bonneville near the curb.

"This is nice," he said, touching the shiny hood. "Once I get my license, you'll see what car I'll have."

"Just get in and put your seatbelt on."

"Where do you want to go?"

"I don't know. You pick."

He gave her directions to a Greek restaurant. "You'll taste souvlaki identical to that of Athens."

"I doubt it."

He bought two sandwiches. After the first bite, Dunia frowned. "It's not the same."

"It's pretty close."

She ignored him.

At his suggestion, they went to a park. Pushing her on the swings, he said she had gained weight. Her feet skidded the ground. "I want to get off," she said.

"Okay, what do you want to do?"

She looked at the sky. "I want to go home. It's drizzling."

"Let's take a few pictures. I brought my camera."

Rolling her eyes, she said nothing. Amel asked a couple passing by to take their picture. He slicked his hair back and posed nobly beside Dunia.

"Get closer," the woman teased, compressing her palms. "Come on, a little more. Ah, you could do better than that."

"You're giving people the wrong impression," Dunia said after the couple returned the camera and walked away.

"It's not their business." He quickened his pace to catch up to her. "I meant to ask you. Do you still have the negatives of our Greece pictures? I want to duplicate the missing ones."

"I gave you a copy of each and every one."

"I sent some to my family in Baghdad."

She frowned. "Which ones did you send?"

He didn't answer.

"Not the intimate ones?"

Lowering his eyes, he smiled.

"Amel, you didn't!"

"What's the big deal? They weren't intimate."

"Me sitting on your lap with your arms around me is not intimate?"

Still smiling, he shrugged. She shook her head and dug into her pocket for the keys. In the car, he turned on the radio and tried to kiss her.

She pushed him away. "We're not going there again," she said. "No way."

Her intellectual faucet turning up, she spelled out the things she hated about him.

"Your persistence, lack of communication skills, inability to protect, defend or understand me gets on my nerves," she said, her veins standing out on her neck. "Your attachment to your family, the broken promises and above all, your selfish love makes me want to choke you."

"Me? Selfish?"

"Your only concern in Athens was that you loved me," she said, driving up to his curb. "'I love you, Dunia', you kept saying. But what about me? Didn't you care that I didn't love you? Didn't my feelings count?"

"Why are you doing this to me, Dunia?" he asked, tears forming in his eyes.

"Get out!" she growled. "Just get out!"

What a beast, he thought, slamming her car door shut and marching inside. And he had intended to invite her in for tea!

He didn't know what had caused the explosion, whether it was the pictures he sent to Iraq, his attempt to kiss her, or the weight-gain comment. Why would that upset her? It was only a few pounds. Maybe it was the test. She had been on edge the minute she arrived. Maybe it was her parents. Having met him, they fully understood, and applauded their daughter's decision not to marry him.

To allow time for her temper to cool down and his dignity to mend, he decided to leave her alone for a while. She called one day, bored. "You call only when you're bored," he laughed. "Deep down I wish you'd always be bored, so you'd turn to me."

"The volume of information in these damn books is driving me insane. I just want to lock myself up somewhere."

"You can come over whenever you like. I'll make a key for you."

"Would you mind leaving me alone if I did come?"

"Not at all."

"I'm serious."

"So am I. But if I left you alone, who'd prepare dinner and tea for you?"

"You can make the dinner and tea, then leave."

"I'll do that."

The night before her test, she called again. "Since you have an appointment with your attorney tomorrow, can I stop by after class? I need a little rest—away from home and everyone."

"Yes, stop by!" he said, hoping his quick response wouldn't scare her off.

She arrived at two o'clock.

"When will you be leaving?" she asked, taking off her jacket.

"I'm not. The appointment is cancelled," he lied.

Annoyed, she headed towards his bedroom. "I'm going to change into something comfortable. Don't come near me."

Amel walked in on her. "At least close the curtains."

"No one can see." She wore the beige nightgown she had on in Athens. She removed her pants and bra, grabbed a book from her school bag, lay on the bed and read.

"I cooked lunch," he said.

"I'm not hungry."

"Are you sure?"

She set her book down and joined him in the living room. He placed two cups of tea and a pan of fried meat and tomatoes on the table. Using pita bread, they wiped the pan clean. Then Dunia returned to his room for a nap. She warned him not to disturb her—she'd had only four hours sleep the night before. He nodded, placed the dishes in the sink and followed her.

"What do you want?" she asked, lying sideways.

Quietly sliding beside her, he started massaging her shoulders. "Leave me alone," she commanded.

He wouldn't listen, so she lay on her stomach and asked for a back rub as well. Soon his massage turned into kisses. She flipped from his arms like a slippery seal, then shoved him away with the heels of her feet.

She grabbed a telephone book from over his nightstand. It was gold with a thick engraving of the Parthenon. "You know," she said, "I never bought a souvenir for myself in Athens."

"Why not? You were out and about all day."

"I don't know. I forgot."

"Yeah, your mind was elsewhere," he said.

She was quiet.

"Why are you suddenly quiet?"

"You're just like your family! You've picked up ugly habits from them..."

"Maybe I've picked up habits from you. I'm around you more than them."

"No, I think it's either from Neherein, Wafaá or her daughter, Susan."

"I barely speak to Susan."

She grinned. "Who knows what the two of you do?"

"What did you say?"

"I didn't say anything," she said, laughing.

He slapped her on the mouth. "You never think about what you're saying. Don't say things like that again."

He pretended to be upset but really, he loved her boldness. He kissed her again. Before it got dark, she checked the refrigerator and decided to eat *biryani.* He warmed it in the microwave, boiled water for tea and brought out a pound cake. She took four bites of the cake, before he told her it was made by Wafaá, and put it down.

"Wafaá made the *biryani* too," he said.

She stuck her finger down her throat.

He served a bowl of fruit. She took a peach and got ready to leave.

"Wash the sheets," she said, eying the bed. "I don't want any evidence for your aunt and sister to see. If they ask you whose hair this is, tell them it's Susan's."

"Why do you talk about Susan that way? She's a good girl."

"I haven't said anything bad about her. Anyway, there's a lot that you don't know."

"You think so?"

She nodded confidently.

She called him later that evening. Her voice was hoarse.

"What happened?" he asked, concerned.

"My mother saw the nightgown in my school bag and accused me of having come to see you," she said. "She never wants me to set foot inside Canada again."

He was stunned. It reminded him of the time in Greece when Dunia called her mother and that same night insisted she move out of his place.

"Aren't you going to say anything?" she asked.

"What's there to say? I'm speechless. I was going to make you ribs next week."

"I hate ribs. I like steak."

"Ribs are better than steak."

"How do you figure? Steaks are twice as expensive."

"It doesn't matter. It's the taste that counts."

She sighed. "Every time we start something, it's shattered. This could be a sign you should find a girl who'll love you and whom you can marry. We're wasting our time together."

"Yeah," he said, dazed. "Well, no problem. We can call, can't we?"

"Yes, of course."

"Good, we'll do that. What about the negatives? Should I send them with Wafaá or maybe—maybe I'll mail them?"

"That would be better. I prefer she sees nothing."

"You could come here with a friend."

"I don't have friends I trust that much."

"So I can't see you until I come to America?"

"Yup."

"You think you'll still be around, or working overseas?"

"I don't know. I'll come on your birthday."

"When is *your* birthday, Dunia?"

"You don't know?"

"I know it's somewhere around Christmas...."

"It's nowhere near Christmas."

"Yes, it is. I'm sure of it."

"What makes you think you know my birthday better than I do?"

"It's in—"

"I can't believe you've forgotten!"

"I have it written down here. I could've sworn it was during the holidays."

"It doesn't matter. I should let you go."

"What will you do now?"

"Study. And you?"

"I'm going to sleep. I won't be able to do anything else. Oh, what a life! It's not pretty."

"I'll talk to you later, okay?"

There was a long silence.

"Dunia, I love you," he said in English.

CHAPTER 20

e sat on a street curb and viewed Wyandote. Amel was devastated that the metro, buses, souvlaki stands and Omonia Square had disappeared. From this far away, the dust of Athen's beauty settled and the gypsies who leaned against walls, breastfeeding their six-year-olds as they extended their pitch-black hands through their soiled veils were now queens passing out strawberries. *Efcharisto* and *parakalo, yassas* and *ochi* were crisp in his memory. The Greek women, so natural, leapt to mind. The men, lucky to urinate behind poles and trees without getting ticketed, had it made. They worked little, sat in cafés, drove motorcycles, dated casually.

With Dunia gone, Amel frantically searched for a hobby. Nothing appealed to him, so he hung around with his classmates. One night, they took him to a bar. He had one beer and an upset stomach. There were Chaldean girls who crossed into Canada for the night because they were too young to drink in the U.S. "They come here to party," one of his friends explained. "No one can see what they're up to."

"No one?" Amel said. "Aren't we people?"

"We don't count. They don't know us, we don't know them."

Amel watched the indecently dressed and heavily made-up girls twist like snakes around men. Their lewd expressions were such an offence to Amel, his lineage and village that he couldn't see straight. He wanted to leave but his friends forced him to stay.

He couldn't sleep that night. America was made of unfamiliar crops and insects. How could he live with it? But it was too late to go somewhere else. Damn that Dunia! Had they teamed up, he would feel strong. She always had an excuse to maintain her distance.

But her mother was right. Why should Dunia waste her time—jeopardize being seen—with a man she didn't love? She'd regret it in the future. Then again, so what? He was a first cousin, not a stranger. Feeling awful himself, he tried to twist her resolve.

"You really don't plan to visit me until I come to America?" he asked.

"It's out of my hands."

"If you really wanted to, you could come."

"I'd have to lie to my parents. I'd rather not do that."

"You don't call anymore."

"First of all, I'm putting in extra hours at the office. Second, I'm working hard in school. Third, I'm tired—"

"Fourth, I miss you very much," he interrupted, "Nothing I do stops me from thinking about you. I can't get you off my mind."

"You ought to get married," she suggested, "A girl with a green card who can both get you into America and help you forget me. Oh wait, a green card won't do. She has to have a U.S. citizenship."

He turned serious. "I'm not thinking about marriage now."

"Oh? Then why were you thinking of it in Greece? Was it appealing there because it meant America?"

"You know very well that wasn't the case. I wanted marriage because I loved you."

"Do you love me now?"

"Why do you ask that?"

"Why do I ask that?" she asked threateningly.

"You will not hear anything nice from me," he said, feeling the tension, "because you don't deserve it. I'll speak and what will I gain?"

"You only say and do things to receive something in return?"

"No, but you like to draw secrets from people and tease them."

"Why don't you marry Susan?"

"I told you, I'm not thinking about marriage. I want to make something of myself and help my family come to America. I don't want to be in a situation where my wife works. I want to make my bride happy, not worried."

"How romantic. Would you consider marriage with me?"

"Why do you ask that? Did you forget what you said when we were in Athens—we don't belong together, ever!"

She was quiet.

"What's wrong?" he asked, thirsting for revenge.

"It doesn't matter what I said at the time. I don't remember it."

"Well, I remember. I remember it very well. It hurt me when you disappeared those five days. Twice I almost lost my hand in the machine at work, thinking about that...."

"Who cares?" she snapped. "Leave it alone. Pretend it never happened."

"No, never. I could never do that. The Greek islands—even if you didn't go—are the ugliest place in my eyes. I never wish to hear of them again. I knew the whole time you had someone—the whole time I felt it."

"Stop it!"

"Couldn't you at least have come up with a better lie? Had you checked, you'd have known the resorts aren't open from mid-September to mid-May. You're usually so smart."

"Usually I am. But whoever gets a hawk at their tail trips."

"The thing about the islands only validated what I already knew."

"So you were smart for once. Good for you."

"Why did you leave him if you loved him?"

"I don't know that I loved him...."

"To run off with him for five days, to hurt me so, you must have. Did he love you?"

"Of course! But it's more complicated than that. Everything is so black and white to you."

"Who was he?"

"Amel..."

"Who?"

"A classmate."

"American?"

"Yes."

They were silent momentarily. "Is that why you two didn't marry?" he asked.

"It's one reason. He also lives in another state," she said. "Is he why you won't say you love me anymore?"

"I say it."

"Hardly."

"Well, you know it."

"If I know it and you know it, why not say it?"

He didn't answer because he wasn't sure why he didn't say he loved her. Partly he was punishing her but also something had changed. It was like his heart had bounced to his forehead. The love he had for her still existed, but now it was a rush of thoughts, not music.

Besides, he wanted someone who loved him. If one of them surrendered it would be a servant-master relationship.

Her Thursday class was cancelled and Amel lured her over for dinner. She was mad that he burnt the steak and had run out of potatoes. He wanted to know how that was his fault.

"You could've gone down the street to buy some," she said. "It's not like you work."

He tried to come up with a good excuse rather than admit he was lazy, but couldn't. "I hate cooking potatoes. You have to peal, slice, fry, scrub the grease...."

"I wanted them baked!"

"So we're having steak without potatoes. Big deal."

"That's not the point." Her face red, she sat down and folded her arms. "I don't think I'll visit you anymore. You've changed towards me."

"I have not."

Staring at the burnt steak, she stood up. "I'm leaving."

"What!?" he cried. "Come on, I'll make it up to you. Please don't go."

For twenty minutes he implored her to stay. In the end, she ate the whole steak and they kissed mechanically. As she hurried out, a nail on the door snared her blouse. She tied the threads to keep it from ripping.

"I'll buy you a new shirt," he said, walking her outside.

"Thanks," she said. "I'll wipe my butt with it."

He grabbed the back of her neck, pinching it.

"What? I can't be honest?"

She nudged him away with her shoulders and swung her hips while getting into her car. Glancing provocatively at him, she started the ignition. He stood firm as she shifted into gear and backed out. In that instant, he fell in love with her again.

Wafaá wanted to sneak him into the U.S., but he refused. He didn't want to get her into trouble: after all, she was blood and married with children. He had accumulated respect for his aunt, who from his first day in Windsor, had been a mother to him, neglecting her own home to supply him with food, clothes and shelter.

In her early forties, Wafaá still possessed youthful energy. Her humor and serenity made her a good caretaker and friend. He was careful never to bring up Dunia's name, but shared his other fears and ordeals with her. She listened to every word.

She brought Amel a box of groceries one evening.

"If you want, I can do your laundry on Saturdays," she said, stacking canned soup in the cupboards. "My kids don't have school, so I can come early in the morning..."

"Aunt Wafaá, I know how to do my laundry. I lived on my own for years."

"Susan and I can stop by on the weekends to clean..."

"What needs cleaning?" he asked, looking around. "I'm one person and the apartment is small."

She turned and stared tenderly at him. "I want to make things easy on you."

"You and my uncles have done plenty for me already."

She began drying the dishes she had just washed. "I don't trust you'll say when you need something, that's all."

"I will. You've provided everything already."

She sat beside him on the couch and touched his face. Her hands were chilly and smelled of Palmolive. "You don't know how dear you are to us," she said. "Your father raised us. We owe him a lot."

Amel bent his head.

"I don't want to depress you. I'd just like to do whatever is necessary to make you comfortable." She lowered her eyes. "Amel, do you still talk to Dunia?"

"I'd rather not say."

"Is marriage out of the question?"

He didn't reply.

"What happened before was a misunderstanding. Had she not asked for the *sougha*, we would have given."

"You don't have to explain," he said, not wanting to talk about the mishandling of the bride price that had messed up his chances with Dunia.

"Yes, I do. I'm sure you had the wrong impression of me back then." She gently pressed his shoulder when he tried to disagree. "It's okay, Amel, I don't blame you. That's not my reason for bringing it up. I needn't say more. You'll know the truth in the U.S."

Soothed by the renewed relationship with his relatives, Amel made an oath to repay them generously when he got the chance. This enthusiasm evaporated when he was alone and he called Dunia. She was adamant about keeping him out of her tent.

"I have a gift for you," he said.

"Give it to me when you come here."

"By the time I get to the U.S., you'll be married."

"I doubt I'll be married by then," she said.

"Maybe not. With your requirements— someone rich and handsome and...."

"I have three years of school ahead of me, which I'll try and finish in two."

"And you have high standards."

"Yes, I do. I want someone unlike you!"

"You want someone like the guy you went away with in Greece?"

"Exactly like him! Exactly like Dan!"

"Quiet, or I swear I'll cut this man to pieces. You and this phantom loser of yours..."

He heard her speaking to someone else in the room. "Darling, Neili, would you want me to marry an ugly man with pointy ears?" Dunia laughed. "She just frowned and shook her head no."

"Who are you talking to?" he asked.

"Neili, my aunt's five-year-old daughter. I'm watching her. Neili, should I marry a poor man? Again no, *habbibti*?" She laughed harder. "Should I marry a dumb man? Amel, she's shaking her head no."

Amel snickered.

"The man you marry must have green eyes," Amel heard Neili exclaim.

"See Amel, it's as if she read my mind," Dunia said. "The phantom had green eyes."

He was a barn on fire.

"I'm sorry," she said, sensing his enormous heat. "I was joking."

"It doesn't bother me."

"Listen, let's write letters until we see each other."

"No. You'll have your mother read them for you."

"I'll read them myself, but keep it brief—a sentence or so."

"I won't write anything."

"How about a postcard?"

"No."

"Please Amel. Write me one word. Even your address is fine."

"I'll see."

"My God, one word, Amel!"

"Okay, I will," he gave in.

"I'll be waiting."

"I doubt you'll wait."

"Don't say that. You have the wrong impression."

"I do?"

"One day, when you're older and smarter, you'll see for yourself."

The next time they talked she was very upset. "I heard your mother is going around Baghdad calling me materialistic," she said. "She says the reason your aunt and uncles didn't want me for you was because I'd asked for a ten thousand dollar ring."

He had heard that rumor once, and knew it was exaggerated. To maintain peace, he hadn't taken sides.

"Did you hear what I said?" she asked. "Now your mother is trying to make me look bad. She's siding with the people who got you into Canada."

He sighed heavily.

"Aren't you going to say anything?" she asked.

"What do you want me to say?"

"What would be the point of telling you what I want you to say?"

He sighed louder. "I have to go now."

He went to the refrigerator and drank a glass of orange juice. His bones felt weak. He would have fallen asleep had the tenants not knocked on his door, calling out, "Fire! Fire!"

He put on his sandals and rushed downstairs. Someone had had a kitchen fire and the back of the building was in smoke. His apartment wasn't in danger but the fire department evacuated everyone and he used this as an excuse to avoid contact with Dunia. He stayed with a friend from class for a week.

He called her two weeks later.

"How could you ignore what I told you for two whole weeks?" she asked him.

"There was a fire here."

"You're lying."

"I'm not. Come look at the building."

"Was anyone hurt?"

"No."

Amel got off the hook that time but he didn't know if she would bring up the subject again. One day Aunt Wafaá called with horrifying news. As soon as they hung up he dialed Dunia's number.

"My Uncle Riyadh had a stroke," he told her. "He's in the hospital, dying. His one request is to see me." Holding back his tears, he choked up. "I want to fulfill his wish."

"Does he even know you?"

"He left Baghdad before I was born."

She chuckled.

"He's still my uncle!"

"It's just that you never mentioned him before," she said. "It's odd he'd think of you on his death bed."

"You don't know how close my dad's brothers and sisters are."

"Can't they bring him to see you?" she asked.

"He's hooked up to machines."

"Oh Amel, I'm so sorry."

"I can't take it here anymore. I want to be with my family. Last night I stood in front of the tunnel entrance and was tempted to jump over the fence to get to Detroit."

"Don't be crazy," she said.

"Aunt Wafaá wants to sneak me in but I'm afraid for her," he said. "Eventually, as risky as it is, I might just have to do it. What did I come here for? I'm as much a refugee in Canada as I was in Greece. I can't work and I'm costing my uncles a fortune in attorney fees."

"Your condition is temporary."

"You don't understand. I'm tired of being separated from my family."

"Amel, I know it's not easy but be patient. America is only minutes away and your uncle might be in the hospital, but he's not dead yet."

The next day his uncle died.

CHAPTER 21

mel sat cross-legged on the curb. Above his head, a red-winged black bird landed on a branch. At his feet, ants scurried along. He dropped popcorn and the ants became mountain climbers. The bird flew away.

Amel observed the people passing by until a guy winked at him. He stood up and dusted off his jeans. He went home and lay on the couch. TV was a haze and he turned it off and lay in the dark. He thought of his family. He cried.

Each day was a ride on a Ferris wheel. He hopped on hoping it would be fun, was ploddingly spun in a huge circle and returned to the same spot, queasy. If it was going to take a lifetime to reach a goal, why bother? He should have remained in Athens, where olive oil, pollution and garbage reigned rather than this sanitized Canadian order.

He missed his ex-boss, Mr. Tree, who had taught him that paper was made with wood, pounded into pulp and rolled into a sheet. His fingers longed to once again lay out, shape and sand wood. Brushing on a flawless finish was like icing a cake.

The phone rang at 9:17pm.

"I'll be over to pick you up at 10:45pm," Wafaá said with determination. "Be ready, got it?"

Tongue-tied, Amel could not, would not argue. He wanted to attend his uncle's funeral after missing the open casket and burial. At least he could pay his respect at the Seventh Day ceremony, held on Sundays.

When they hung up, he read 9:25pm on the VCR. Tonight was his last night in Windsor. He watched for his aunt from the living room window. Why had she said a quarter to ten? Did the tunnel close and if so, would he miss his chance if she came late?

Wafaá arrived in a red van he had never seen before. Her daughter Susan waited in the passenger seat while his aunt came in alone. Dressed in black stretch pants, a Las Vegas T-shirt, house sandals and gold jewelry, she looked like an ordinary Chaldean. In reality, she was a pillar accustomed to hard weather and holding up others.

"Susan, Peter and Michael are in the van," she said. "You sit under the seat cushions. We have two stops, the first for the toll, the second for customs. If everything goes okay, which it will, we'll be done in a minute."

Amel nodded. Before they walked out, she told him to leave the kitchen light on. There were greetings when he entered the van. The boys ate ice cream cones and Susan had a bag of peanuts in her lap.

"Go to the back," Wafaá said. The back seat opened like a coffin. He squeezed in and it was shut. No one said a word as the van moved. Five minutes later, they stopped, and a moment later they continued. Amel's sweat was as sticky as caramel.

The van stopped again.

"Citizenship?" he heard a man say.

"U.S.," his aunt replied.

"Where were you born?"

"Me, Iraq. My kids in America."

"Can she roll down her window, please?"

"Susan," Wafaá called, but her daughter had already followed instructions.

"What were you doing in Canada?" he asked slowly.

"Took my kids to a Chinese restaurant we like there—Ho Wah," Wafaá said.

There was a pause. Amel's heart dropped to his stomach.

"I need proof of citizenship," the man said.

There were paper shuffles and mumbling.

"Here's their birth certificates and here's my passport."

"Bringing any gifts?"

"No."

"Alcohol, drugs, weapons?"

"No, nothing."

A long pause followed.

"Alright, go ahead," the man said.

The van moved.

They stopped within minutes and Wafaá told him to get up. "You and Susan stay here while I return the van to my friend," she said. "Sit in one of the restaurants. Susan, you have money?"

Susan nodded and Wafaá gave her a cellular phone in case of an emergency, then drove away. Amel observed the busy street with Greek names and music. "Where are we?" he asked Susan.

"In Greek Town."

Dunia had mentioned the neighborhood before. He asked Susan if he could borrow her phone. She showed him how to use it and he called Dunia. "Guess where I am?" he asked. "That place where they do *oupas*. My aunt snuck me in."

"You're kidding!"

"I'm not. Listen." He held up the cellular towards the *sagonaki* flames. "Dunia, I'm here! Can you believe it? You're the first to know."

"Congratulations, Amel," she rejoiced. "A thousand congratulations. Who's with you?"

"Susan."

"Really?" she jumped. "Now you can start a romance in Athens part II."

"Wait until I get a hold of you."

"If you do."

That night he was up until 5:00am trying to contact his mother, but failed. Sunday morning Wafaá's son Michael took him for a haircut and to buy mourning clothes. At the church hall, Amel did not sit—he served coffee, unfolded chairs, helped set up the buffet, and picked up napkins.

Dunia's parents were at the funeral, but she was not. Uncle Jabir came all the way from Arizona and made a point of discussing business matters with him, promising to hire the best attorney for his case. Uncle Basam, who owned a gas station in Detroit, offered to train him once his English improved. Wafaá suggested that in the meantime, he work as a stock boy at her husband's store.

"I want a word with you," Wafaá said, pulling him to the side. "See that girl?"

He followed her eyes. There were nine rows of girls dressed in black.

"The one in the left corner, her hair up in a bun," she said. "The one with silver jewelry – about seventeen years old—a wide face."

It was a fat face. "Yes, so?"

"Her name is Elizabeth. She's an excellent girl. Her mother is my best friend."

Amel was confused.

"She was born and raised here, but with an Arabic upbringing," she continued. "She knows how to be a hard worker and a good wife."

He frowned. Now that he had made it to America the last thing he had in mind was to be tied down. He finally had dreams for himself, of establishing his own business and uniting his family. Besides, she wasn't his type. In a group of females, she would be the vase and they the flowers.

The girl turned around and glanced shyly at him. Her cheeks were big and red as plums.

"Have you said anything to her?" he asked.

"Not really. She heard of you from her mother. What do you think? Is she pretty?"

Amel huffed and puffed.

"If you change your mind," Wafaá said, patting him lightly on the back, "let me know and I'll introduce you."

"Okay, thanks." He didn't know what else to say.

Relatives paid their respects at Wafaá's house until midnight. Amel cleaned and put the furniture back and didn't get to bed until 3:00am. He shared a room with Michael in the basement—the lowest level of a pyramid for the living.

He woke to the smell of fried beef and tomatoes. Staring at the ceiling, he felt old resentments trickle through his muscles. He recalled the past days' events and wanted to expunge every bad thought he had had about Wafaá. He exalted her for having struggled for his sake. What had occurred between her and Dunia faded from his consciousness.

After breakfast, Wafaá took her children to Windsor to empty out Amel's apartment, giving him a chance to call Dunia. "When can I see you?"

"How are we supposed to go out when you don't have a car and you live with your aunt?" she asked.

"You can pick me up down the street."

"Never. If anyone sees me, they'll imagine I'm chasing after you."

"No one will see. It'll be dark."

"No, thank you. I've brought enough gossip on myself as it is. I don't want any more."

While drinking two and a half cans of Minute Maid, he came up with a solution and called her back. "What if we meet at the mall? My cousin Ayad can drop me off."

She complained that the mall was too public, but in the end she reluctantly agreed. He arrived first and browsed in the stores, then twiddled his thumbs in Burger King. She was ten minutes late. They left before anyone noticed them and went to Big Boy's. She ordered fries and he had a Coke.

He called the waitress over, remembering the movies. "Thiz ize too much."

The waitress couldn't understand him until he repeated himself several times. Once she left, Amel checked out the plants and booths. "This restaurant isn't much," he said, imagining the luxury in store for him.

She didn't say anything, and he figured she was thinking, 'big shot already?'

To camouflage his haughtiness, he complimented her outfit: a white shirt and short black skirt. "Where did you get the top?"

"Here, in the mall."

The waitress brought a glass of Coke with less ice.

"Your skirt is from Greece, isn't it?" he asked. "I remember we bought it together. It doesn't look very good, though—sort of makes your stomach stick out."

She jabbed a French fry in her ketchup. "What do you know? You have no taste."

She tapped her fingertips against the napkin, tore the edges, then excused herself. While she was in the bathroom, he stole four of her fries. She returned to the table and stood in silence.

"Aren't you going to sit down?" he asked.

"I want to leave."

He sipped what was left of his drink and took out his wallet. "I should only give a fifty cent tip."

"It's not her fault your English is so bad," she said, walking ahead.

Amel's job offers were placed on hold for one reason or another, so he was home alone most of the time. Wafaá ran errands and visited friends while his cousins attended school, his sister didn't have a car, and his next appointment with his attorney was in a month.

He turned to Dunia, who did one of two things, teased him or taught him history: Margaret Bret was the first woman lawyer in America in 1638; Mumbet was a slave who went by the name of Elizabeth Freeman and who, in 1783, entered a Massachusetts court on her own and demanded her freedom.

"A massage?" he asked, confused.

"Massachusetts!"

His stories were of Athens, of what had happened after her departure. He told her about

Sabah's disco life and Dutch girlfriends, Faris' weight gain, and Hakeem's job as a sweeper. Once he made fun of his ex-roommate Hussam's love affair with a Muslim.

"Why is that a joke to you? You of all people should know what it's like to love," she said. "It makes me wonder. Would you have loved me regardless of my religion or nationality?"

"You can't expect me to answer that."

"Why not?"

He wasn't comfortable with her tone and ignored the question. She wouldn't drop the subject.

"So tell me, would you or wouldn't you accept me no matter what?"

"What are you hinting at?"

"Say for instance I wasn't a virgin."

Blood rushed to his head.

"Would your love stay the same, Amel?"

He wanted to knock this stupid boldness out of her.

"Tell me, Amel," she insisted. "Would you still worship me if that was the case?"

"I don't know!"

She laughed with sarcasm. "I'm not surprised that's your answer. It makes me miss Dan, though. He didn't put conditions on his love."

He restrained himself from lashing back. He hated it when she put on her lawyer face, interrogated him and sentenced him harshly for minor mistakes. He wondered what made her so hostile and why she stuck around. Was it his love for her or was she bored? It was neither. It was because the other man, the right man—maybe this

Dan—was not available. If he were, she would be gone.

They agreed to take turns calling; she on Sundays and he on Thursdays. As it worked out, he called her every day. The day she learned she had scored high on her LSA's she invited him to *Beauty and the Beast on Ice.*

"I can't go anywhere. I'm in mourning."

"Your Uncle Riyadh died over a month ago."

"It's only been twenty-nine days."

"That's close enough."

"No, it's not. It's like breaking your fast early."

"But we're not going to a party. It's a show, like watching TV."

"It's an outing, so it's disrespectful towards my dead uncle."

"Grief is in the heart, not in keeping yourself from an ice capade."

"It's public. What would people say if they saw me there?"

"No one we know goes to these things, trust me. Even if they did, you're not a girl. You're not expected to fulfill all forty days of mourning. Besides, Wafaá, your uncle's own sister, who's married with children, has been going out and about from the first day he died."

He hated this attack on Wafaá's name, but to avoid an argument, he didn't comment.

"Tell me, is she home now?" she asked.

"She left late this evening for the church shrine in Ohio that Chaldeans go to once a year," he explained, careful to clarify Wafaá's intentions. "She's coming back tomorrow morning."

"Oh, she can't miss that, can she, prayerful as she is?"

He held his breath. Despite Dunia's plea, he was against going to the ice show. She got agitated and said goodbye but called back within minutes. She greeted him softly and he was happy that the tension had broken.

"I called back to tell you a story," she said. "Once upon a time, there was a girl who wanted to specialize in International Law. She did, became successful at it, got married, had kids, the end."

"But this same girl once said she didn't want to stretch her stomach by having babies."

"That was before she fell in love and changed her mind."

"Oh, so now she's in love?"

"She is—with Stephen, Bashar, Quais—the list goes on and on."

"Funny, this same girl mentioned something about staying chaste even after she marries...."

"Stop it," she said emphatically.

He laughed. "Do you remember saying that?"

"No!"

"I know you do."

"I was trying to make a point—how badly I didn't want anything to interfere with my dreams."

"Your dreams! Bah!"

"You won't say that when I'm working in an embassy in some European country and you'll need me to grant a visa."

"I'll visit you at your home overseas."

"As what?"

"As a friend."

"That won't be a good idea."

"I'll come with my wife and children."

"You move awfully quick."

He ignored her remark. "My boy and your daughter will meet and have a romance."

"No, I'll never allow that!"

"Why not?"

"Never with your son."

"You won't be able to do much to stop it—if you even know about it."

"I will know about it."

"How?"

"I'll be very close to my daughter. I'll warn her about your blood type..."

"It's the same as yours."

"I'll change mine."

"But if they fall in love, you won't..."

"I won't let her!"

"Fine, then I'll tell my son not to make a big mistake and fall in love with your daughter."

"He'll ask why."

"I'll say it's because she takes after her mother—she doesn't know how to love."

"Amel, who do you love?" she asked sweetly.

"A girl named Dunia. She drives me crazy."

"Does she love you?"

"No," he said.

"Why not?"

"I don't know."

"Maybe she just can't say it."

"She doesn't have to say it. I'd feel it if she did."

"Do you think she'll ever love you?"

"I doubt it."

"And if you, my friend, know she doesn't love you, why are you still after me her?"

"Because her voice and face bring me peace and comfort."

"The girl in the story—she told me about you."

"What did she say?"

"Things..."

"What sort of things?"

"That you love her dearly."

"And what else?"

"That you'd die for her."

"And what else?"

"That you love her more than you love your own life."

"What else?"

"That's all."

"Did she tell you why she doesn't love him?"

"Because he's an immigrant. He can't afford her."

"You can't place a price on love."

"She's not that type of girl. She charges."

"Really? That's news to me."

"It's a trend in America for Chaldean girls to charge. Maybe she'll make an exception for first cousins."

"There are no exceptions."

"Of course there are."

"Quiet!" he said, unable to listen to more.

"It's two in the morning," she said, her voice fading. "I have to get up in four hours."

He begged her to talk a few more minutes.

"How much do you love me, Amel?" she asked drowsily.

"More than my life. I'd die for you."

"What else would you do for me?"

"What else is there to do?"

"You love me, Amel?"

"You know I do." She stopped asking questions. "I will not come to your wedding, Dunia. Remember that. Don't bother to send me an invitation. I'll feel very terrible when you marry. Will you come to my wedding?"

"Of course," she yawned. "I love parties, dancing—I might meet someone."

He took a deep breath. "I'll get married in this country and nowhere else. Maybe I'll bring a girl from back home." He paused. "Oh, I can't do that, can I? I don't have a green card. Anyway, I want two kids and that's it."

He sensed she had dozed off, so he stopped talking. Closing his eyes, he envisioned his prospects: a white picket fence, a Jaguar and Lamborghini, being the owner of the largest warehouse for all metropolitan party stores. Good thing he hadn't married Dunia. He would have been too young and unaccomplished. She was too strong and career-oriented.

CHAPTER 22

afaá called him into the kitchen late at night. He was in his pajamas and everyone else was asleep. She took a pita loaf out of the freezer and told him to sit down. Leaning against a chair, a coffee cup in her hand, she asked how well he knew Dunia.

"Very well," he said.

"Is she honorable?"

"More than any girl I've met."

"Then why don't you get married?"

Caught off guard, Amel didn't answer. Dunia's face appeared and, for an instant, he relived their joys and difficulties.

"Is she untrustworthy?" she asked.

"No!"

"Are you two on speaking terms?" She sat down and observed him closely. "Why do you maintain a relationship if you won't marry?"

"I don't want to marry anyone right now."

"Why not? You love her." As he lowered his eyes, she persisted, "Does she love you?"

"Why are you asking these questions?"

"Because if you continue this attachment, it'll ruin you. It's senseless. Think about it, Amel. How do you plan to stay here if not through marriage? The lawyer can't guarantee you a green card. He can only elude the courts for so long before you're deported. He's charging hundreds a month.

Multiply that by years, and it amounts to a down payment for a house."

"Once I get a job, I'll return every penny my uncle spent on me."

"It's more complicated than that. Your stay here is considered illegal. If you're caught working, the business will be fined."

That had never crossed his mind.

"Amel, having a wife will secure your residency and speed up your learning and financial progress. Give me one good reason to remain single. What benefit is it to you, who likes stability?"

He sulked. How could he once again approach Dunia about marriage after all he had said? She would grill him until she got the facts. She would be convinced that his original plan to marry her had to do with coming to America. She would hate him forever.

"And what about your family in Baghdad? If you marry now, you'll have citizenship in three years. Then you can start your parents' petition." She hesitated. "I know a girl—my friend's daughter—the one I pointed out to you at the funeral, Elizabeth. She's a sweetheart and smart too...."

He turned his face to the wall.

"Amel, hear me out. This girl knows your troubles and wants to help. She's willing to drop out of high school to marry you. She's a saint."

"We're talking about marriage not church," he said. "Besides, she looks older than me." Hugging himself he tapped his foot.

"That's not the reason I called you in here." She shifted her chair closer. "I'd prefer not to get involved, but in case you're thinking of a future with Dunia, there's something you must know.

You're new to this country, and as long as I'm your aunt, it's my duty to help you see clearly." Pausing, she sighed deeply. "Amel, Dunia has terrible secrets concerning men and money."

She spoke as softly as a bird sang. Her words shook him. He tried to sort things out in his mind but couldn't and his confusion neutralized his temper as she finished her speech. He went to the basement and dialed Dunia's number, trying to open the subject immediately. She talked determinably of how a professor gave her the wrong date for a test.

"Why do you sound so odd?" she asked, although he had made no comments.

"Dunia, how long have we known each other?"

"Over two years."

"If I ask a question, you'll tell me the truth?"

"Of course. What is it?"

"The things you said the other day—the other men—are they real?"

There was a chilling silence.

"Amel, who talked about me?" she asked sternly.

"That's not the point."

"It is the point. If I know who talked, I'll know why they said it."

"Dunia, is it true?"

"You dare ask?" she sneered. "You, who have known me for years, ask who I am? Who talked about me?"

"I can't say."

"Is protecting them more important than defending me?"

"They have nothing to do with it."

"It's your aunt, isn't it?"

"No, you don't know them."

"If I don't know them, then they don't know me."

"They know of you."

"Give me their names."

"I can't."

"They must be family. Otherwise, why would you protect or trust them so much?"

"They have nothing to gain by lying."

"They're turning you against me, aren't they?"

"Dunia, they have details. They know the names of the men you mentioned on the phone—Stephen, Bashar, Quais."

She pondered. "Someone is setting me up. They listened in on our conversation."

"How could they do that, and why?"

"Two of the men I mentioned were made-up."

"They say they have proof."

"They have proof?" she asked, stunned.

"There are witnesses, willing to confront you."

"They'll say it to my face?"

"Yes."

There was a long silence.

"You're already convinced, aren't you?"

He was. He knew from Athens she had it in her to seduce men. Dunia hadn't been the same since he arrived in Canada. She was modest and reserved; she brought up marriage when she didn't love him. Now he understood. She wanted to hide a scandal. Once he discovered the truth, it would be too late: he was family and would never divorce her.

All along she had pretended to think badly of Chaldean men, when really, aware of her reputation, they had no choice but to act how they did with her. She used her education and ambition to veil her faults, so initially it was difficult for them to unfold her identity. When they figured her out, they fled. No wonder she felt more at home with American men, famous for their compassion towards loose women.

"Have them come and see me," she said. "But one last time, Amel. Who talked about me?"

"I can't say."

"You will never hear my voice again."

"I can't say."

"They're that dear to you?"

"I'm sorry, Dunia."

Amel went upstairs. His aunt was in the living room watching Jay Leno. He stood in front of her, exhausted. "Call those people," he said. "Dunia wants to confront them."

Wafaá's face turned white. "What did you do?"

"I told Dunia everything."

Her lips and hands trembled. "Why didn't you consult with me first?"

The ground was suddenly uneven beneath his feet.

"My God, Amel, how stupid of you! Why did you tell her?"

He looked at her in disbelief.

"There are no witnesses!" She stood up, her coffee cup tilting and drops nearly spilling. "Your conversation the other day was recorded. When she said what she said, I thought she meant it. I wanted to test you, to see if you're aware of her true character. I suspected this was why you didn't want to marry her."

He was out of his mind. If handed a rope, he would have hung himself, a knife, he would have stabbed the walls. Given a Q-tip he would still have done something violent.

"I have a self-activating tape recorder in my bedroom. It's hooked up to the phone jack. I press one button and it picks up three hours' worth of phone conversation. It was intended for my children, but—Jesus, Amel," she cried, sitting back down. "How could you tell her?"

The telephone rang and, controlling the rhythm of her breathing, Wafaá answered. It was Dunia's mother.

"Amel? Yes, he's here," she said, eying him briefly. "But why don't you tell me what you want? I can resolve your problem better."

Amel's life was over. The puzzle he had been putting together was thrown upside down, and all the pieces shuffled.

"I know about it," Wafaá said. "Come to my house tomorrow morning. I'll explain everything." She listened a moment. "It's not that, Moneera. Please, come over and you'll understand. Yes, fine, bring Dunia."

She hung up the phone. "They're coming at nine. Moneera says you'd better be here too."

"I'm going to the store with your husband," he said. "You have to clear my name by yourself."

"Her mother won't let you off that easy. She'll drive to the store and straighten you out. I suggest you stay."

He returned to the basement feeling like a ball of dough. Wafaá had beat him, kneaded him and broken him off into pieces. He couldn't sleep for feeling like he was being rolled into pretzels.

At 8:00am, he moved around the bed like a caged wild bird. He then went into the bathroom and vomited. The doorbell rang at nine o'clock. Amel rushed to the living room to claim a seat and catch his breath before Dunia and her mother walked in.

As the voices came towards him, the pangs in his stomach hardened like cement. His aunt appeared first, then Aunt Moneera, and last, Dunia. Dunia's face was a mustard color and grave, her eyes were small from fatigue.

"Hello, Amel," Aunt Moneera said quietly.

Dunia didn't say a word as she sat close to her mother on the couch. Amel was glad they faced the blank TV screen and not him. Dishes and silverware clinked in the kitchen. Everyone was quiet and avoided eye contact until Wafaá came in with a tray and set it on the table. She invited them to taste her pastries and asked if anyone took milk in their tea.

Aunt Moneera inquired if the meat pies were bought or homemade. The latter, Wafaá answered proudly. Moneera complimented them and Wafaá offered to make breakfast.

"No, thank you," Moneera said kindly. "We're here for an explanation. Start Wafaá. Open the subject that kept me up all night."

"Before I begin, know that what happened was unintentional. There's this tape—"

"Am I speaking with Amel?" Dunia interrupted, laughing knowingly.

"Yes," Wafaá said.

"Is that it?"

"Let me finish."

"No!" Dunia said. "Is that it? Because if it is, I've said whatever you heard. Is this over now?"

"Dunia, wait a minute," Moneera said.

"Mom, I told you it was her! She taped our conversation."

"Where is the so-called proof?" Moneera asked Wafaá.

"The cassette tape," Wafaá said.

"Amel said there were witnesses."

"Because he's stupid," Wafaá said as if Amel was the Las Vegas ashtray on the coffee table. "When I approached him with this subject, I wasn't expecting him to call Dunia."

"What did you expect him to do?" Dunia's voice quivered. "Take your word and hate me?"

"You wanted to blacken my daughter's name?" Moneera asked sadly. "We've known each other for as long as my sister has been married to your brother. There was love between us."

"Allow me to explain, please," Wafaá said.

"And you, Amel," Moneera interrupted, looking with disgust and hurt at him. He was hunchbacked, timid as a kitten. "You ought to know Dunia and you were fooled just like that." She snapped her fingers.

The room was silent. No one came to his defense; no cup accidentally dropped or broke. He lowered his head in shame.

"Please, Moneera, listen," Wafaá said. "I went with my sisters-in-law overnight to a church shrine in Ohio. As I always do in order to safeguard my children's whereabouts and the type of friends they are with, I set up a tape recorder to record all phone calls."

"If it was intended for your kids, you should've pressed stop when you heard our voices," Dunia said hotly. "You had no right listening in on us."

"This is my house and I can do whatever I wish in it."

"You don't have the right to invade people's privacy," Dunia said and her mother nodded in agreement.

"In my house I do."

"Then you have no shame." Dunia was so angry Amel wanted to crawl back to the basement before anyone took real notice of him.

"Really Wafaá, what was the purpose behind that?" Moneera asked more calmly.

"I was trying to get to the bottom of Amel's heart. When I ask him what is going on between him and Dunia, he won't answer. His uncles and I want them to get married. It's better than getting the run-around by attorneys and he doesn't know how difficult his case is. But he won't marry. I thought his doubts stemmed from not knowing Dunia well enough."

"You think Amel doesn't know me?" Dunia asked. "I suppose that's why he loves me to death."

There was more silence while Amel suffered the embarrassment of having his personal feelings passed around like sunflower seeds. He saw Wafaá's eyes lock onto Dunia's as she took her in with pique.

"Before we go further," Wafaá said, turning to Moneera, "you should be aware of the type of language your daughter uses."

"No, I shouldn't," Moneera said. "A young lady flirting on the phone with her boyfriend—who happens to be her first cousin—is common."

"To my husband I don't say half the things she said."

"Of course not. Couples needn't talk about the things they do. You think if what she said was true she would tell it to his face?"

"I don't know how she could talk that way at all."

"You don't? Pass out these tapes to the Chaldean community. See if people are more surprised by two lovers, cousins flirting, or by the boy's aunt having recorded the conversation and listened to it."

"She slandered me too," Wafaá complained. "She said I didn't sit home once since my brother died."

"Out of this stupid comment you conspire to ruin me?" Dunia's lips and eyes twitched. "You don't know how much harm you could have done. You have a daughter not much younger than I."

"I didn't aim to harm you, Dunia," Wafaá said, touched. "I swear on my children's lives, I only did what I did to see Amel's response. I didn't know the idiot would call you so fast. If he was a man, he'd ask to see the proof first."

"You're right, he's not a man," Dunia said, "which is why I was reluctant to have him as a husband. If he was a bit smart, he'd known a well-off virgin wouldn't sleep around for money."

Up until now, Amel was happy that no one seemed to notice him. Now he felt as important as the eggs in the refrigerator, replaceable if smashed. No matter how lame his excuses might be, he had to speak if ever he wanted to look at himself in the mirror again.

"Dunia, my God," he said awkwardly. Everyone fell silent, as though a bird just flew in from outside. "I admit my behavior was immature, but has nothing I've done counted?"

Dunia frowned. She almost started to speak but restrained herself.

"I love you," he said, prompted by her wavering. "You were my world, my life. I would have died for you." He looked at her hard. "My love for you is still my passion."

She looked away without a response or reaction. An injured insect would have received more sympathy from her, but he was not willing to give up.

"Dunia, I'm sorry. I should've—" He rubbed his forehead, then concentrated, choosing his words carefully. "I know I saw everything in black or white or on or off, rather than gray, the middle, the balance. I know my love was often lopsided but I had no idea...."

He dropped his vehemence to catch his breath. Looking at Wafaá, he clenched his teeth. "I was raised to be honest. I expected the same from everyone," he said. "Next time I'll research things myself."

Wafaá, primly composed, placed her teacup on the table. Amel felt by their heavy stillness that Dunia and her mother were satisfied with his apology. Dunia's foot twitched. He couldn't tell whether she was anxious to leave or tell him off. He hoped for the latter. At least then they would be speaking.

"You couldn't have meant it when you said you'd never speak to me again," he said, looking at her left profile. "I don't believe it."

"Excuse me," Dunia said to Wafaá, uncrossing her legs. "May I use your restroom?"

"It's the first door to the right," Wafaá said, caught off guard.

Dunia left the room and Amel's voice wrapped itself up again. He would never get her back. She had made that clear by publicly pouring the final insult over him.

She returned shortly afterwards and sat down beside her mother. Nothing had been said or done in her absence. Both aunts had stared at the carpet to spare him from further humiliation.

"Perhaps what I did was wrong," Wafaá said as if she had been hit by brick. "But I didn't have bad intentions."

Dunia laughed with sarcasm.

"Honest, Dunia, I've never had a thing against you."

"We're no fools," Moneera said. "We knew from day one you didn't want Amel to marry Dunia. You can't sit here and say you did when everyone knows you didn't."

"It's obvious you hate me," Dunia said. "I can tell from your eyes. I don't want my name ever again pronounced on your lips."

"I swear I care for you," Wafaá said. "I promise to honor your name as I would my sister's. I only ask that, please, none of what occurred be mentioned to your father."

Dunia refused to promise anything.

"I'm sorry, Dunia," Wafaá said. "Really, I am." She faced Amel and her lips parted slightly. She turned away. Evidently the hurt in his eyes muffled her words.

"We'll leave now." Moneera picked up her purse from the floor. "It's unfortunate it's come to this. I hope it's never repeated."

"Never!" Wafaá said. "I'm washing my hands of this subject. You can have the cassette if you want."

"We do want it," Moneera said.

Everything was still when Wafaá disappeared. Amel could hear Dunia and her mother's thoughts of him: when it comes to class, you and your relatives can't beat us.

"Here you are," Wafaá said, placing a tape the size of a pack of gum in Moneera's palm.

"From this day..." Wafaá kissed Dunia on both cheeks. "I'll treat you as a sister and I ask that you do the same with me."

She tried to catch Amel's gaze, but he avoided her eyes. He couldn't stand the sight of her face and her voice gnawed at his bones. He wished he could remove his belt, tie her ankles and throw her in front of traffic.

Pardons and blessings were said upon parting.

"Bye, Amel," Aunt Moneera said as she walked out.

Dunia didn't say a word to him. Wafaá walked them to their car and Amel hurried back to the basement and covered himself with a blanket. Minutes later he heard footsteps coming down.

"Aren't you going to eat?" Wafaá asked.

He was wiped out. Nothing, not even food, could relieve his agony.

"They blew the whole matter out of proportion. Wafaá, what did you say? What did you say? How could you say this?" she imitated. "Why doesn't Dunia look at herself?"

What a coyote!

"As for you—my God, Amel, if you've never slept with the girl, how could you believe what I said?"

Shaking her head, she stomped upstairs.

He was bed-ridden for a month. Unable to express his pain to anyone—to protect both Dunia's and his aunt's reputation—he thought he'd die. Someone would have to loan him their sanity before he recovered, but whatever he needed to release, he would have to release himself. He had to in order to gain strength and move out.

CHAPTER 23

amily, friends, a chocolate cake and an elaborate lunch awaited him. It was his aunt's idea to celebrate his twenty-second birthday at her house. Uncle Jabir had called from Arizona earlier to wish him a happy birthday. His mother called him as well, and somewhere after their long greetings, she urged him to obey his Aunt Wafaá.

"She says she has the perfect girl for you," she said. "Don't be picky, Amel. Your opportunities are thinning."

"*Youm*, you have no clue what goes on here."

"And you don't know what's good for you."

"*Youm*, please!"

"How is work at your uncle's gas station?"

"It's decent. He has a bigger heart than the rest."

"You shouldn't have moved out of your aunt's..."

"*Youm!*"

"Wafaá has the ability to see and hear clearly..."

Fortunately the line disconnected.

He left his apartment for a drive in the white Sable Uncle Basam had helped him buy—he had paid half of the four thousand dollars. Getting his license was easy, since he had driven in Baghdad and he had a translator on the written test. But avoiding a ticket was hard. He was caught speeding and was ticketed for parking next to a fire hydrant.

Financially, Amel was able to afford Guess jeans, a stereo system, and a pager. He sent his family in Iraq clothes and shoes. He had a three-hundred dollar weekly salary and shared his five-hundred dollar a month apartment on Schoehnner Road with a cousin on his father's side, also an immigrant who his uncles helped smuggle into America.

When Amel returned, he checked his answering machine to find his sister asking for the fourth time where he was. "Amel, come on. We're going to blow out your candles without you."

What a potato chip, he thought, hating Neherein with a passion. She epitomized self-indulgence and drifted through life with a dreamy look upon her face, doing little to help him adjust to America. She had allowed Wafaá to snare him in her web.

He put his feet on the table and turned on the TV, glancing at the phone. For months he had been calling Dunia at work and listening to her 'hellos' until she eventually hung up. Today was different; he had to speak to her and vent his frustrations. Otherwise, the whole apartment complex would feel a blast from his furnace.

He dialed her number, hung up before anyone answered, then went outside for fresh air. Sitting on the curb, he cracked the wedges of pinecones like rose petals. So much depended on how Dunia reacted. She would either lift him from his misery, or bury him alive.

He had tried to write her a letter, but knowing she wouldn't respond, he didn't finish two lines before he threw it away. As time passed, speaking to her became more crucial. Hints to marry were politely served like tea by his relatives. Did they think him stupid? He knew that although they could afford it, they no longer wished to fund him.

Amel felt like an old piece of furniture in a garage sale. Maybe he could still turn things around. His knees grew soft as clay before he stopped his daydreaming and went inside. He picked up the phone and listened to the dial tone. He hung up.

He tried again, hung up and decided to go see her. He called the main line and asked the receptionist for the address.

The drive to her office—listening to Arabic music with the window open—was calming until he parked. Suddenly he felt very cold. The office was a house, coated in grapevines. Amel looked in his rearview mirror, straightened his hair and checked his eyes. He didn't want to go in looking scared. Taking a few deep breaths, he went in.

An African-American woman sat at the front desk. "Can I help you?" she asked.

"Is Dunia in?"

"Yes, whom shall I tell her?"

"Her cousin."

The woman wasn't gone twenty seconds before Dunia appeared behind her. Her smile vanished when she saw him and Amel's legs and lips quivered like a moth against a light bulb. They greeted each other formally. She asked him to follow her into her cubicle.

"So you're starting law school next month?" he asked.

"Yes," she said, her back to him as she saved something in the computer.

"I'm happy for you."

"Thank you."

She turned and faced him. The silence was uncomfortable.

"Sit down," she said, motioning to a chair.

"You know Sabah made it here?" he asked nervously.

"I heard it cost your uncle ten thousand dollars."

"The first smuggler deceived him."

"Oh? Your uncles still buy people entry into America in order to own them," she muttered to herself.

An older blonde woman walked in. "Dunia, I'm sorry to bother you. I know I should know this by now, but damn it, I can't get it right. When you're registering a letter, do you..."

Laughing, Dunia took the outgoing mail from the woman's hand. "I'll do it for you, Pauline." She stamped and sealed a paper over two envelopes.

"You're a sweetheart. Bye." She waved to Amel.

The phone rang.

"Excuse me," Dunia said, "I have to get that."

Removing her left rhinestone earring, she picked up the receiver. Amel watched as she tried to reschedule a court date for her boss. Her flowing hair was tinted with henna. She wore navy and cream striped pants and navy blouse. She was attractive and professional. He remembered her playfulness in Greece and imagined her having her own business one day.

She hung up the phone.

"I have to take this stack of files into my boss's office," she said, putting her earring on again. "I'll be quick."

"Go ahead."

He made room for her to slide between him and the wall; she smelled of jasmine and fruit. He wished he could touch her, even if it was only her fingernail. She went across the hallway, where a small dark-haired man in his late forties sat behind a big desk. Amel observed her cubicle. Postcards and news articles hung on the wall, and on her desk was a clock the shape of a book, a crystal ball with a sailboat and water inside, a plastic goldfish holder on her papers and Lifesavers. There were no pictures.

Dunia returned, scanning some papers. "What else is new?"

She hadn't once sat down. She was probably more edgy than she appeared.

"Dunia, can we be alone a minute?"

"No one can hear us if you keep it low. Besides, you're talking Arabic."

"I want to talk in private."

She sat down and brought her chair closer. "I can't leave."

He didn't know where to start. The atmosphere didn't help. People were walking back and forth in the hallway and she could get a phone call at any time. He pushed himself to speak. "Dunia, I want to explain myself."

"Amel, don't," she quickly reacted.

"Don't what?"

"I don't know. I can't digest speeches of how much you love me anymore, or how sorry you are."

"You don't want to talk to me?"

"It's not that," she sighed. "I'm just sick of problems." She looked down. "If your aunt, an obvious enemy of mine, fooled you so easily—my first cousin and friend—I'm better off with a stranger."

"She wanted me to hate you so badly..."

"I know. You and your family almost destroyed me. The day after we all met, I couldn't get out of bed. Is this what the love you boast about does to a person?"

"Dunia...." He paused. "Can you forgive me?"

"Forgive you? I don't punish people for life, Amel. You're the one who wanted to remember what I did with whom and how. So what if I'd spent time with another guy? It was in the past and I didn't break any promises."

He couldn't defend himself.

"It all happened for the best," she said with conviction. "We were never compatible. Time proved that over and over. We remain cousins, always. Nothing more."

He cleared his throat.

"You know the funny thing?" she asked. "Partly what kept me in your life after I left Greece was our story. I thought there was more to our relationship than met the eye. The picture I sent to Baghdad and our time in Greece kept me thinking what we had was special—"

"It was! It is."

"No, it isn't," she said firmly. "In Greece you placed your family first and here, you acted like an emperor. I hated it. I was always ready to flee, but you duped me by your compliments and romantic gestures."

"I was sincere, Dunia," he said, although he started to feel defeat.

"It doesn't matter. Stories can be changed, everyday."

The phone rang, and they turned towards it.

"I'm not going to answer that," she said, glancing at the flashing number.

He took the opportunity to change the subject. "You know, the necklace I gave my nephew got lost."

"Really? That must have upset you."

"Very much."

"How ironic," she said softly. "The day you had your aunt ask for the necklace, you broke my heart. I wore it night and day." She fell into a daze. "It was so long, it curled over my notes in class and spread on my pillow at bedtime. I loved having it against my skin because it had your aura."

There were tears in his eyes.

"I'm glad God took it away," she said, collecting herself.

"I did so many stupid things."

"Me too."

"You don't hold a grudge against me?"

"No. It all happened for the best."

"Why do you keep saying that?"

"Because it's true. My mission is to get a law degree and go out with it into the world. You won't be able to walk with me."

His pager went off. He saw his aunt's number and ignored it.

"Do you need to use the phone?" Dunia asked.

"It's not important."

"Go ahead, use it. I have to make some copies. Dial nine first."

She left and he called his aunt's house. Neherein answered, full of scorn for being late.

"Cut the damn cake without me."

"Amel, don't be a baby. Hurry. The guests…"

"I don't care about the guests," he interrupted. "Tell them to go home."

He hung up and blocked out everything Dunia had just said. It was their first conversation in half a year. What tactic could he use, he wondered, to get her to give him another chance? She returned with a folder.

"I'm sorry, I didn't ask if you wanted anything to drink," she said.

"I'm fine. Are you sure we can talk here? You won't get in trouble?"

"I'll bring you something cold."

She left and returned with a Pepsi for him and coffee for herself.

"I was thinking," he said, pulling himself together as he popped open the can. "Let's go to the library one day. You used to want me to gain knowledge?"

A few drops of coffee leaked from her mouth as she drank. She grabbed a Kleenex. "We'll go, but we can't be seen alone. I don't want anyone to mistake us for a couple."

"Is that so?" he asked, trying to be humorous. "Who would you bring along—your parents?"

"You can bring your fiancée or someone."

"My fiancée!"

She casually wiped the rim of her cup. "Yes. She and I might become friends."

He was confused; she was giving and taking all at the same time. "I'm not engaged."

"You will be."

"And you believe I could introduce her to you just like that?"

"Why not? Are you going to pretend I never existed?"

Her teasing, almost cruel, robed him in grief.

"I told my fiancé about you," she said.

"You're engaged?" he asked, all the threads in his fabric snapping.

"Not yet, but I will be soon."

He searched for a question to ask, a comment to make. He was angry and wanted to pour water over all her paperwork. "Is he Chaldean?"

"He's Ukrainian."

He didn't know what to say. Was that African, European, Asian or what? He placed his arms against his stomach to preempt the ache.

Her face softened. "If there's one thing you helped me do, it was to let go of my limitations. With my career, the sky's the limit. With men, I lessened my options—mostly for the sake of culture."

"I wish I never did that for you."

She laughed. "It wouldn't have worked. No matter what, even in keeping my honor, I don't fit the Chaldeans' mentality. I've realized since that as long as I know my heritage and my partner knows his, we should be fine."

He was too sad to look at her or drink his Pepsi. She might as well have shot him.

"What will you do today?" she asked.

"I'm going to my aunt's. They're having a birthday party for me."

"Oh, happy birthday! My God, I forgot."

"I don't want to go," he said. "I actually thought of skipping it."

"Don't be silly. Go and have fun. Don't hold a grudge against them."

She was done, he thought. She had rinsed herself of him.

"I'm sorry, Amel, but I have to get back to work. Keep in touch, okay?"

Crossing her arms, she smiled widely and stepped back a few feet.

As he walked out of the law building, his body stopped as though it had died—like during a sneeze, when heartbeats cease and the brain doesn't function. Some said that in that instant, the soul left. Not sure if it would return, they said, "God bless you."

As he revived, time wavered and his obsession with Dunia curved into a circle. The image of his aunt and her contrived innocence disgusted him. She had done one good thing for him—she had smuggled him into the U.S. and he was thankful for it. Then she balanced it out with one bad thing, which he would never forgive. She did the first in order to have the power for the second.

He was surprised to find himself at Wafaá's doorstep.

Everyone rushed to greet him. Sabah was there, a plate of food in one hand, vodka in the other. "Man, you dummy," he said, grinning. Man was the only English word in Sabah's vocabulary, repeated in almost every sentence. "You missed the best part, man. Your cousin, Ikhlas, was belly dancing alone in the middle of the family room—barefoot and all."

Amel glanced at Ikhlas, who was helping clear the kitchen. She had on a tight leopard print dress.

Sabah burped. "What's the matter, man? Hey, sorry I couldn't get you a gift. I got to Kmart and realized I left my wallet with my roommate. I swear, man."

Amel looked hard at Sabah. He was exactly the same as before, but with less hair. Amel wanted to put a bucket over his head.

"Listen to this," Sabah said, nudging his elbow. "A Kurd, whenever he walked a certain path, fell into a ditch. Each time he managed to get himself out. He said he'd try it one more time and if he couldn't get himself out, he'd walk back home."

"Sabah, my love, get yourself barbecued wings," Wafaá said, taking Amel by the arm. "Come here, Amel. You finally get to meet my wonderful friends."

She introduced him to Elizabeth and her mother, who were sitting quietly in the far corner.

"Hi," Elizabeth said.

Amel nodded. There was nothing else to say so he excused himself and sat down. From the corner of his eye, he observed Elizabeth. She was as red as the first time he saw her at the funeral. Her bland eyes to the ground, she wasn't twenty percent as pretty as Dunia, nor could she ever come close to having Dunia's glow. Her mother was so petite and pretty that she could pass for her sister.

Wafaá brought him a plate of chicken and stuffed cucumbers. "What do you think?" she asked, winking.

"She barely talks."

"She has manners."

He faked a smile. Elizabeth didn't sway to brilliance or darkness. She was in the middle. Maybe she had the potential of full bloom.

Reclining in his seat, Amel began his journey of independent thinking. He detached himself from his emotions and contemplated the situation. Dunia's radiant tresses were as distant as the moon and her wit and knowledge had to be filed away. He could never grow with her. He could never catch up.

Many obstacles stopped him from making a marriage with Dunia, yet he fought against them. Why, with all the signs to the contrary, did he continue to cling to the idea of her?

He wanted a girl who would feel like home. He needed someone who would solve problems in the same way as he did, not look down on him, not try to correct him—someone who would say she loved him. But if he and Elizabeth married, would one of them eventually outgrow the other?

"Don't imagine how the two of you will get along during good times," his Aunt Wafaá spoke, calling on her saintly side. "Imagine how you would be together during hard times."

He already missed Dunia terribly. They had a history; she was his aunt's daughter, his first-love, his memory of Athens. She was a flower. Yet the beauty and splendor of the flower required care, and lasted only a week or two. Elizabeth was a vase. She could be decorated and if treated properly, survive for decades.

Sabah tapped on his shoulder. "Come cut the cake, man. We want dessert. The jello is melting."

A drip kept hitting against Amel's chest.

"Leave it alone," he said to himself after having tried to wipe it away.

As he tired of its thorny stems and fallen petals, the flower began to wither. But could he forget the memories and emotions attached to its fragrance? He was afraid, and wanted to be held. The vase could contain him. There, he would release his history, embellish his present and craft his future.

THE END

الكاتبة الأولى في التاريخ المدون كانت أمرأة من العراق القديم تدعى انخيدونا . قضت انخيدونا (الكاهنة الكبرى في معبد الإله القمر ننار) حياتها بالتأليف والتعليم قبل حوالي ألفي عام من ظهور أرسطوطاليس ، وسبقت سابفو بألف وسبعمائة عام .

أن العجلة (الأختراع الأكثر أهمية في تاريخ البشرية) وغيرها العديد من الإبتكارات مثل شبكة أنابيب المياه والمحراث والزورق الشراعي ، كلها قد أبتكرت في بلاد ما بين النهرين .

الشعب الذي كان في الماضي قد ساهم بشكل عظيم في تأسيس حضارتنا ، تقوم ونام نعمو اليوم بتصويرهم ، كما أنها تشاطرنا برواية أخرى يومية معاصرة ترتكز على أحداث حقيقية .

حٔڝڗ̈ܝܠܐ ܬܘܿܡܝܼܠܐ ܝܬܝܗ ܝܝܚܕܘܢܐ ܚܠܝܒܬܐ ܡܬܡܐ ܒܚܡܐ ܡܚܒܬܢ

ܓܠܟܪܒܬܐ ܚܠܟܝܡܐ ܝܒܕ̈ܐ ܥܢܚܪܐ ܐܕܘܒܝܚܘܢܢܐ ܡܘܢܝܒܐ

ܥܢܕܪܗ ܚܘܠܪܘܿܣ ܕܡܠܟܘܢܐ ܘܢܬܡܬܢܐ ܚܠܝܬܐ ܡܝܒܪ ܡܬܝܡܝܠܗ

ܠܠܗܡ ܝܠܚܕܬܐ ܠܐܠܩܝ ܥܝܬܐ . ܡܚܝܒܪ ܡܓܝܩܗ ܕܘܠܩܐ ܠܐܗܝܐ

ܠܡܚܐ ܥܝܬܐ

ܠܘܝܟܕܬܐܠܗ ܡܬܐ ܡܝܢܕܝܒ ܠܝܒܥܢܐ ܚܝܥ ܡܚ ܠܠܝܡܚܐ ܠܠܝܚܕܢܚܡܠܐ

ܘܠܐܡܪܗ ܚܢܝܒܬܐ ܡܚܝܕܬܐ ܢܝܠܐ ܓܘܗܝܠܓ ܚܘܒܪ̈ܝܠܐܕ ܡܚܢ

ܘܡܚܚܡܠܐܕܝܚܝܒܢܐ ܘܡܝܬܐ ܚܡܐ ܘܓܡܢܐ . ܚܘܒܠܪܘܣ ܥܝܒ ܟܥܢܠ

ܚܝܒܘܓܐ ܚܠܐܗܒܬܐ ܕܝܒܠܝܒܪܘܬܝܗ

ܠܘ ܓܡܠܐ ܕܐܘܓܢܐ ܢܡܚܢܐ ܓܘܝܠܟܘ ܚܢܝܒܬܐ ܝܚܕܬܐ ܡܗ ܠܐ

ܕܡܬܕܘܡܝܠܐ . ܘܝܚܬܐ ܠܐܘܝܘ ܢܡܬܐ ܡܠܐܝܚ ܢܚܡܗ ܕܡܝܪܗ ܕܠܝܪ ܪܠܝܪ

ܠܠܝܠܓ ܕܝܚܢܠܐ ܕܠܐܥܚܒܝܡܠܐ ܡܝܗܡܠܐ . ܚܚܝܒܬܐ ܠܠܝܝܚ ܥܪܠܐ ܕ ܒܠܟ ܝܚܝܒ ܠܐ
. Mardo ܚܒܢܘܡܠܐ

Arabic and Aramaic translation by:
Gorgees Mardo

HERMIZ PUBLISHING, INC.

Pick up a copy of Namou's previous novel, The Feminine Art
Also available in Arabic

ISBN 0-9752956-1-6 (hardcover)
ISBN 0-9752956-0-8 (paperback)

ISBN 9959-30-079-X (paperback – Arabic Edition)

Available at most local bookstores
Amazon.com
Or by calling 1-800-214-8110

www.HermizPublishing.com

Look for Namou's upcoming novels

THE UNRIPENED HEART – a story of a young Iraqi lady's struggle between her eastern heritage and western lifestyle and her journey towards a sense of belonging.

MY BROTHER'S WIFE – a young widow finds herself regressing into her restricted girlhood status after her husband dies, and starts to fear there's no chance for a second romance.

A MIRROR OF TWO BROTHERS – a Palestinian Christian girl falls in love with a Tunisian Muslim and must choose between him and her family and town.

VIDEO CASTLE – Namou's memoir, centered around the video store she worked at for 12 years, shares her personal schooling experience.

The Mismatched Braid
Available at most local bookstores
To order, visit our website at
www.HermizPublishing.com
Or call us toll-free 1-800-214-8110
(credit cards only)